I0638582

MORE THAN WORDS

Trickle Creek: The Lyons
Book 2

ELENA AITKEN

Trickle Creek

<u>The Lyons</u>
From Grumpy to Forever
More Than Words
Fake It 'Till We Fall
Best Friend Trap
Only For Tonight

<u>The Carlsons</u>
Never Let Me Go
If I Can't Have You
Always Be Mine
Because You Loved Me
Keep On Loving You

More Than Words

*Starting over was the goal—falling in love wasn't.
I came back to Trickle Creek to build a life for my
daughter, not fall for the uptight bookstore owner
next door.
Delaney Hart shuts me down at every turn—but I
can't stay away.
And when a snowstorm traps us together, all bets
are off.
She thinks I'm like her ex.
She's wrong.
Because I'm not walking away.*

Chapter One

Ethan

"There is no better sound in the world than an old wall coming down."

The next swing of the sledgehammer landed with a satisfying crack, and plaster crumbled in chunks around my boots with the large hole I'd just put in the wall. Dust filled the air, thick enough to choke on. Somewhere behind me, my brother muttered something under his breath.

"What was that, Reid?"

I turned to see him shaking his head. "I was just saying that I can think of a lot more satisfying sounds than destruction." He raised his eyebrows and gave me a pointed look, which I ignored.

Just because he was happily married to a sexy wife he couldn't keep his hands off, didn't mean the rest of us were.

Or that it was something we wanted.

At least, it wasn't something *I* wanted. A relationship was so low on my radar for the moment, it didn't even register. I had enough to keep me busy. Like destroying the wall that stood in my way of an open concept room.

I'd keep my focus on demo, thank you very much.

I lifted my sledgehammer and swung it again, rewarding myself with the solid crunch of the old wall.

"Careful you don't hit something important," my handyman brother, who truthfully had a lot more experience with this kind of thing than I did, muttered. "I don't need my to-do list getting any longer than it already is." He pushed past me and reached into the hole I'd just made to pull out a big piece of plaster. "Remind me again why you didn't hire someone for this?"

"I did." I wiped the sweat off my forehead with the back of my arm. "That's why you're here."

"Funny." Reid shot me a look. "I don't remember any discussion of payment."

"That's 'cause there isn't any." I flashed him my most charming grin, not that I thought for a second it would work on my younger brother. "It's the family special."

Reid grumbled a little more under his breath. Something about a *special* still requiring some form of payment. But I knew he was happy to help. Despite his crusty exterior, my grumpy brother was a softie. Especially for his family.

And I wasn't ashamed to cash in on that generosity.

Not when I was desperately in need of help if I planned to ever open the doors to Peaks & Brews.

I had way too much to do to turn the old Chinese restaurant—which had been sitting empty in the plaza for longer than I could remember—into my new brewery space as soon as possible. I'd more or less signed my life away when it came to the lease payments, so the sooner I could start making money, the better.

And I was confident I *would* make money. As soon as the

walls were down, and we scrubbed the lingering scent of deep-fried ginger beef out of the air, we could get the tanks in and move operations out of my backyard shed and get things going for real. It was long past time to turn my home-brewing hobby into something real.

Something that would give me and Quinn a solid future.

My little girl deserved that more than anything.

But first, we needed to get past the destruction stage. And judging by the state of things, it was going to take a fucking miracle. Or a lot more work.

"I still think we should keep the dragon mural on the far wall." Reid wisely changed the subject away from the extra money I didn't have. "It adds character."

"You just don't want to paint over it."

"You're not wrong." Reid chuckled. "But seriously, it does add character."

"We'll see." I glanced at the mural. It *did* have character. But I wasn't sure that a 1983 over-the-top Chinese food restaurant was the vibe I was going for.

"Seriously, whatever it is you decide to do, Ethan, it's going to be great." Reid set his sledgehammer down and watched me from across the room. "This place has been sitting empty for too long. It'll be good for the whole town for something to fill this space." It was unusual for my brother to offer up any kind of positive reinforcement at all, and I was just about to mention that fact when he finished his thought. "As long as the fancy beer you brew isn't total shit."

"Asshole."

I tossed a chunk of plaster at him, but he dodged it easily with a laugh.

"Wait and see." I set my sledgehammer down and crossed the room to where I left the cooler of beer. Not my brews—yet. But soon, if everything went according to plan. "This place is going to be great. It's long past time for Trickle Creek to have a brewery." I tossed him a cold can. "But it'll be more than that. It'll be a place to gather."

Reid cracked the tab on his can and lifted it in cheers before taking a deep drink. "I look forward to that day, brother. Truly."

I nodded my appreciation. Traditionally, my brothers and I didn't do a whole lot of emotion. At least, we tried not to.

Instead, I turned and surveyed the space, looking past the mess to see the vision.

"There'll be a little stage over in the corner there where we can host open mic nights and some local artists." I pointed to a stack of boxes and garbage bags that were ready to go to the dump. "Over there, I'll have some high-top tables for smaller gatherings, and of course, the long bench tables there."

I spent the next few minutes showing Reid my plan, and it was only after I was finished that my brother looked at me with a flash of respect in his eyes. "You're really serious about this, aren't you?"

"Fuck, man. You know I am." I tipped the can and drained the rest of my beer. "It's been a rough road with the divorce and dealing with Quinn's mom. We need this. Both of us. And Quinn deserves to see me build something solid. Something that's *ours*. A fresh start. For both of us."

Reid opened his mouth and for a moment, I thought he might even say something. But then, in true Reid fashion, he swallowed back the rest of his beer and picked up his hammer again. "Well, we better get a move on then." And before either of us could get any more serious about it all, the sound of crunching plaster and splintering wood filled the air again.

Delaney

I'd tried to be patient. Really, I had.

But there was only so much one person could take, and I'd about hit my limit.

For the first few hours, I tried to tell myself that the hammering next door was just temporary. That the floor-shaking thuds and bangs and occasional bursts of laughter and cursing would settle down. For a moment or two, I'd even managed to convince myself that my customers wouldn't notice the incessant racket coming through the old, thin walls.

But by the time my fifth customer in a row commented and shot a wary glance at the wall I shared with what might as well have been a demolition derby next door, my patience had officially run out.

My mystery book club group was due to gather in the next fifteen minutes, and I could still hear the pounding and crashing of plaster next door. I mean, how many walls did they have to knock down over there? The sound wasn't just distracting—it was completely impossible to ignore. Like a jackhammer at the base of my skull.

I stared at the wall between us, my jaw growing tighter by the second. My fingers clenched around my favorite mug, with the peppermint tea I'd brewed in an effort to calm my nerves long since gone cold as I tried to figure out a way to handle the situation.

Ignoring it and wishing it would go away hadn't worked out the way I'd hoped.

Or at all.

The reality was, my little bookshop had a neighbor now. For better or for worse. In this case, definitely worse. And I was going to need to figure out how to manage the situation.

It was either that or throw a book at someone's head. But somehow I didn't think that would get me the result I was looking for.

Confrontation wasn't my style. I was the type who sent carefully worded emails and baked apology muffins for bumping into someone. For years, I'd been the one smoothing things over, apologizing for everyone else, especially my ex-husband and his endless string of bad behavior. Back then, keeping the peace meant keeping myself small.

But that was then.

I wasn't that person anymore.

And this wasn't just bothersome noise—this was my business.

If the new guy next door thought he could just roll into town and put a brewery of all things next to my peaceful little bookshop without any regard for his neighbors, he had another think coming.

Plot Twist was all I had. I wasn't going to let anything happen to it.

Not without a fight.

Not that I was looking for a fight. Ugh. The very thought of that made me want to be sick. With any luck, he'd be a reasonable human who would work with me to find a solution that kept us both happy.

Yes.

If I approached him in a reasonable, calm manner, I'm sure everything would work out.

Still, my stomach rolled at the idea of the unavoidable confrontation.

I took a breath and backed up from the rickety old front counter so quickly, it almost toppled over.

With a silent curse, I mentally moved *fixing the counter* to the top of my to-do list. Not that it would help me get to it any sooner.

"Okay, Delaney," I said to myself. "You can do this."

I tugged my oversized sweater tighter around me like armor.

Time to be brave.

Or at least fake it well enough to get through the next few minutes.

I hadn't been in Trickle Creek for very long, and I still didn't know a lot of people. At least not many I'd call a friend. I'd been so focused on starting up the shop and building it into a business I could be proud of—and pay my bills with—that there wasn't much time for leisure activities.

Everybody I'd met so far had been beyond welcoming of me and so supportive of the shop. So really, I didn't have any reason to be nervous as I left the comfort and safety of Plot Twist and went next door to what had once been a Chinese food restaurant.

According to the few people I'd asked, the shop space had been vacant for almost fifteen years. It was good for the town to have the vacant storefronts filled with new businesses, and it spoke to the recent revitalization the town had undergone.

Trickle Creek had once been a mining town, and when the mines shut down and so many people lost their jobs, the town's future had been uncertain until businessman Michael Carlson had come along and seen the untapped potential for tourism. Over the span of a few years, the ski hill had been improved, a golf course had opened, and new condo units had been built.

What was once a town on the decline had become a thriving little vacation destination. It was the main reason I'd chosen Trickle Creek to be my new home and the base for my bookshop.

That and it was on the opposite side of the country from anyone who knew me, or my ex.

The door was propped open, so I stepped inside, instantly blinking against the dust and noise.

My shoes crunched over debris as I carefully picked my way through the mess. And then I saw him.

Bent over a pile of wood, muscles flexing under a thin gray T-shirt, he looked up at me through a thick lock of hair that had flopped over his eye.

He stood slowly, wiping his hands on a rag as he turned toward me. The second our eyes met, something sparked deep inside a long-forgotten part of me.

Something hot and entirely unwelcome.

He smiled like he knew me.

"Hey," he said, his voice deep and easy. "You must be Delaney."

"Delaney Hart." I blinked and narrowed my eyes. "How did you know that?"

He shrugged, unbothered. "You own the bookstore next door, right? I've seen you around."

That should have creeped me out, but it didn't. Instead, it only annoyed me.

"Well, seeing as you know who I am already, I'm surprised you didn't come introduce yourself before interrupting my day." I jutted out my hip and crossed my arms over my chest. "Since you've been watching me, you may have noticed that I run a peaceful, quiet business that doesn't involve a lot of sledgehammers."

I shot a look at the offending tool propped up against the wall next to him.

His grin only deepened. "Fair. But I'm on a tight timeline. The work needs to get done. And the noise bylaws prohibit me from doing it in the middle of the night."

Never mind the fact that my tiny apartment was upstairs from my shop. I'd never sleep again.

I didn't bother to offer up that little piece of information.

"I have a book club starting in a few minutes."

"And you want me to shut it down."

"I want you to be considerate of your neighbors." I'd been nervous from the moment I heard there was a brewery moving in next door. Construction noise was one thing. But rowdy patrons who'd been drinking all afternoon were another thing entirely, and not exactly conducive to a peaceful, quiet reading sanctuary. I really hoped that this wasn't a precursor to how things were going to be once they opened.

He wiped his hands again and walked toward me slowly —not threatening, just…confident. Like a man who didn't rattle easily.

Like a man who was used to getting what he wanted.

I knew that type.

"Look," he said when he was close enough for me to see his rich-chocolate eyes. "I know it's loud right now. And I really am sorry, but there's no other way to do demolition and construction. I have permits and like I said, a lot of work to do before I can open my doors."

"Which I assume will bring even more noise and chaos." I knew I was in danger of being a bitch, but I couldn't seem to stop myself. Something about this man got me off-balance.

"I don't plan on running a nightclub, Delaney."

His use of my name reminded me I still didn't know his.

"I hope not…"

"Ethan." He held out his dusty hand. "Ethan Lyons. It's nice to meet you."

I glanced at his hand, but kept my arms crossed until he withdrew it with a cocky wink.

"Look, Ethan. I like things quiet. Predictable. And so do my customers."

He tilted his head, his eyes scanning my face as if he were trying to solve a puzzle. "Yeah," he said softly. "You strike me as the type who likes things in a certain way."

I stiffened. "And you strike me as someone who thinks he can charm his way out of anything."

"Guess we're both observant." He laughed, full and warm, and for a split second, I hated how good it sounded. "How about this?" he said before I could reply. "Let me know when you have book club meetings and I'll do my best to keep the noise down during those times."

It was a good compromise. Probably the best outcome I could hope for. Still, the way he was looking at me as if he expected me to be grateful for his basic decency got my guard up.

Don't be unreasonable, Delaney. He's not Ken.

"Thank you." I uttered the words begrudgingly, completely aware that I had now fully entered bitch mode and needed to calm down. I blew out a breath and tried to soften my voice. "I'd appreciate that."

He flashed his bright smile in my direction as another man walked out of the back room, an armload of broken plaster in his arms.

"Delaney, right?" The man nodded in my direction. He looked a lot like Ethan, only instead of the overly charming smile, his lips were pressed into a scowl.

"Does everyone know who I am?"

The man shrugged and dumped his load in the corner of the room. "Small town. I'm Reid, Ethan's brother, who's been conned into slave labor."

"More like payback for living in my house and using my shed as your workshop for free until you finally found a woman to fall in love with."

Reid glared at his brother, but I could see the affection between them through the thick layer of grumpiness. Instead of replying, he turned to me. "Sorry about the noise."

"We've reached a neighborly agreement," Ethan jumped in. "I'm sure this is only the start of what will be a fabulous relationship."

I doubted it.

"Don't try to charm me."

"Not trying," he said easily. "Just being friendly."

Exactly.

That was the problem.

Chapter Two

Delaney

The bell above the shop door jingled, but I barely heard it over the buzz saw whining next door.

I closed my laptop and pinched the bridge of my nose. There went my plan to update the Plot Twist newsletter in peace. I couldn't even think, let alone concentrate, with all the noise next door.

It had been three days since I went to introduce myself to Ethan and hopefully strike some sort of deal about keeping the level of noise down.

Not that it had worked.

Sure, he'd taken a break during the mystery book club meeting, and when I asked whether he could keep it down for the mom-and-tot's story hour the day after, he'd refrained from using his saw. But the hammering still came through loud and clear. Most of the kids had been more interested in the sounds next door than they had in the hungry caterpillar looking for his next meal.

"At this point, I should be handing out hard hats with

every new book purchase," I grumbled.

"Okay," a familiar voice said. "But I'm not sure it'll go with my outfit."

I looked up to see my friend Lauren Westfield. She was dressed casually in a flowing skirt and tight tank top with an oversized knitted sweater completing the look. She gave me a sympathetic smile and handed me a little paper bag.

"Here. This might help."

I peeked inside to see a baggie of dried herbs and a sleek, cobalt-blue roller bottle.

I lifted my head and raised a brow in question.

"Calming tea," Lauren said with a laugh. "I made the blend myself. And the bottle is a special mix of essential oils. It should help with focus and tension relief. Roll it on your temples, take a few deep breaths, and try *not* to imagine taking the hammer and throwing it through the wall."

I offered her a weak smile and reached for the roller bottle. "It's worth a try. But no promises."

Lauren wandered over to the front table, trailing her fingers along the new arrivals I'd displayed. "Any luck with Mr. Sawdust next door?"

I groaned and rolled the little bottle over my temples. An aromatic blend of lavender and peppermint filled my senses. "He said he'd try to work around events, but there's been nonstop hammering. I know he has a schedule, too. I really do. But…" I inhaled deeply and reapplied the roller. "Story hour yesterday was basically a dramatic reading of *The Very Loud Construction Site*."

Lauren snorted. "That might actually sell better than the original around here."

"Don't give him any ideas."

My new friend turned back toward me, resting her hip against the checkout counter. "Ethan's not a bad guy, you know. All of the Lyons are pretty decent. I'm sure if you talk to him about it a bit more, he'll work with you. Eventually."

"Eventually isn't going to work for my book clubs and toddler groups," I muttered, rolling the bottle across the inside of my wrist. "Those groups are a huge part of my business, and if I can't provide a quiet and relaxing place to meet…well… I can't think about what will happen."

Lauren offered me a sympathetic smile. "I'm sure all this noise is temporary," she said. "Once the construction phase is over, things will settle down. Brody was telling me that Ethan has a pretty tight timeline to get things ready for his grand opening."

"Brody, huh?" Temporarily distracted, I wiggled my eyebrows. I'd only known Lauren a few months, but our friendship had formed quickly. As far as I knew, she wasn't dating anyone, but she did seem to spend a lot of time with Brody Lyons, who I now knew was Ethan's oldest brother and owner of Peak to Path, an outdoors shop at the other end of the plaza. They didn't appear to be dating, but there was definitely something between the two of them.

"He was helping Ethan out the other night with some painting," she said smoothly, either ignoring my implied question or missing it altogether. "And speaking of Brody, I have to run. He's supposed to stop by and take a look at a crooked shelf. If I'm not there, he'll start reorganizing my tea by mood."

"Mood?"

She shrugged. "Either that or by the color of the box."

"That's…weirdly charming."

"It's definitely weird." She laughed and added, "Try the tea." She glanced at the roller ball in my hand that I hadn't stopped applying. "And if you need a refill of the oils, stop in anytime and I'll hook you up."

I thanked her as she slipped out the door, the bells jingling in her wake, and for one, miraculously blissful second, the shop was quiet.

And then the door opened again.

"Hey, bookstore lady."

"Hey, back." I couldn't help but smile at the girl.

Quinn.

Her long, dark hair was pulled up into a messy ponytail, her backpack slung over her shoulder, and her hands were stuffed into an oversized hoodie.

She'd been in at least once a week for the last few months. Always with a sharp eye for whatever new books I'd recently stocked and an even sharper wit.

"You again," I said with a smile.

"Got anything new that doesn't totally suck?"

I tilted my head. "Depends. You still on your dragon kick, or are you ready to branch out?"

The girl grinned as she wandered toward the used shelf. "Dragons are pretty classic. But I'm open to explosions or something juicier."

"Juicier? You're twelve," I said, teasing gently as I joined her near the shelf.

"I'm very mature for my age," she shot back with a smirk. "Ask anyone."

I didn't doubt it for a second. I pulled a well-loved paperback off the middle shelf and handed it to her. "This one's got a bit of everything. Dragons, age-appropriate steam, and a twist that made me yell."

Her eyes lit up as she took it from me. "Nice. How much?"

"You can borrow it," I said. "Just bring it back when you're done."

In all the time that Quinn had been coming into the

store, she'd never bought a book. Normally, she just pulled one off the shelf and curled up in a chair, speed-reading until closing time. Not that I minded. In fact, she kind of reminded me of myself at her age.

"Seriously?" Quinn blinked up at me, surprised. "For real?"

"For real."

"Okay." She grinned. "But I'm going to give you an honest opinion when I bring it back."

"I wouldn't expect anything less."

She started toward her usual spot, already absorbed in the book. Before I could stop myself, I asked, "Do your parents read, too?"

Quinn paused, but didn't look up. "I don't know. My dad's always busy working. And my mom...she's not really around."

Just like that, my heart gave a little tug.

"Well," I said softly, "you're always welcome to hang out here. Anytime."

She turned and smiled at me. It was just a flicker, but it was real.

Without another word, she settled into her chair and lost herself in the book. The saws and hammers from next door started up again, but instead of letting them get to me, I lifted my wrists to my nose and inhaled the scent of lavender and peppermint.

Ethan

I shoved the door open with my elbow, doing my best to balance the tray of drinks and not drop the paper bag of burgers and fries. "Dinner of champions," I called out as I walked through the small house.

Quinn padded into the kitchen moments later. "Please
ll me you got fries."

"Do I *ever* forget the fries, kiddo?"

She shrugged and rolled her eyes. "You forgot your own
birthday last year, so…"

Fair point.

I dropped the bag on the counter and started to unpack
it while Quinn grabbed plates. As I reached for the ketchup
and mayo, something on the kitchen table caught my eye. A
dog-eared paperback with a cracked spine and dragons on
the cover.

"What's that?"

My daughter glanced over her shoulder. "Please tell me
you've seen a book before, Dad."

"Smart-ass," I muttered. "It doesn't look like a school
book. Where did you get it?"

"The bookstore," she deadpanned. "You know, the store
where they sell *books.*"

"Attitude." I gave her a warning glance. My daughter
was sassy and smart, but that sass could tread dangerously
close to attitude from time to time if she wasn't careful.

"The bookstore lady let me borrow it."

"Delaney?" I turned back toward the food, but the
image of my neighbor in the plaza flashed through my
mind. Big, green eyes. Calm voice that only barely hid a
spark of fire beneath her quiet, controlled exterior when
she'd shown up in my construction zone with that polite, but
no-nonsense tone. She'd looked like she wanted to murder
me…nicely.

"She's cool," Quinn said, sinking into her seat at the
table with her plate of greasy food.

A familiar shot of guilt hit me. It was the third time this
week I'd picked up burgers and fries from the Shed. I really

needed to get better at preparing healthy meals, or at least, grabbing something different.

I made a mental note to place an order from Willa's Whisk, across the plaza, next time to add some variety to our diet.

"Oh yeah?" I tried to sound casual, but Quinn shot me a look, letting me know it wasn't working.

"Yeah." She squirted a dollop of ketchup on her plate before adding mayo to the pile. "She lets me hang out and read. She doesn't hover or act weird like most adults. She gets it."

I wasn't sure what exactly she *got*. But I didn't think it was wise to ask.

Quinn swirled a fry through her mayo and ketchup concoction. I reached for the bottles, making my own mixture of dip, just the way we both liked. But my thoughts didn't move on from Delaney as quickly as they should have. I didn't usually think twice about women I met around town, especially not attractive women who got under my skin in an unfamiliar way.

That was a rule I didn't break.

Ever.

But there was something about her.

Maybe it was the way she tried not to look rattled when she came over, when she was clearly uncomfortable. Or the way she worked to make a deal for some kids' reading hour.

Or maybe it was the way my daughter clearly thought she was *cool*. And had lent Quinn a book?

Delaney *was* cool. She hadn't been trying to impress me or flirt her way through our conversation the other day. She'd just been…real. It was refreshing. Different from what I was used to.

I shook off my thoughts and reached for a fry. "Just

don't take anything without asking, okay? Borrowing is fine, but—"

"Dad," Quinn stopped me. "Relax. She offered. It's fine."

I snorted. But I knew it was. Quinn was a good kid, and she liked to read. There were a whole lot of worse things she could be doing at her age.

And I was certainly glad she wasn't doing any of them.

We ate in comfortable silence for a few minutes, but my mind kept circling back to the woman next door and the fact that, despite how busy I was with the brewery, and balancing that with fatherhood and…well, life…there was something about Delaney I couldn't get out of my head. And that was not good. Not even a little bit.

Quinn crunched into another fry as her phone lit up and binged with an incoming message.

"No phones at the table," I said, but she'd already reached for the device.

Her face clouded over as she read the message.

Forgetting my own rule, I asked, "Everything okay?"

"Just Mom." She shrugged. "Said she'd try to call this weekend. Meetings, blah blah, deadlines, blah blah."

I nodded and worked to keep my tone neutral. "At least she's trying."

Quinn didn't say anything. I didn't press the issue. I'd learned that lesson the hard way. Polly had let her down more times than I could count, and although I'd never said a bad word about her mother in front of her, Quinn was smart. She didn't need me to say what she'd already figured out. She knew who showed up for her and who didn't.

And it broke my heart.

I gathered up my messy burger and attempted to change the subject. "Hey, if you want to, you're welcome to come by the brewery this weekend and help me paint." My daughter gave me a withering look over her burger, making me laugh. "Okay, fine. You don't have to. But don't forget about family dinner at Uncle Brody's this Sunday."

"No way will I forget about the opportunity to have real food."

"Are you saying my cooking doesn't count?" I pretended to look offended.

"It's kinda hard to say that when you haven't cooked in weeks, Dad."

"Fair." I nodded toward the book sitting next to her before I took a bite of my burger. "Is it good?"

She nodded. "It's awesome. Kinda dark but in a really cool way."

"Delaney recommended it?"

"Yeah." Quinn looked up. "She picked it out just for me. She knew I'd like it."

I smiled to myself, letting that bit of information settle. I hated to admit it, but I had no clue what kind of books my daughter would like to read.

I focused on my burger again and took another bite, trying not to picture the bookstore owner next door with her calm voice and quiet strength choosing a book just for my kid, but the image snuck in anyway, taking up space in my brain without permission.

Oh yeah, Sunday dinner with my family couldn't come soon enough. I needed a minute to breathe and clear my head.

Chapter Three

Delaney

Sunday mornings were sacred. The shop didn't open until noon, which meant I had a few blissful hours of quiet without stocking inventory, answering calls, or greeting customers. Not that I minded any of that. Quite the opposite. But still, it was nice to have a break.

Plus, I needed the opportunity to go over my financials without interruption.

As an extra treat, the incessant buzz of power saws also seemed to have ceased for the time being. It was just me, a cup of the tea blend Lauren had given me, and my spreadsheet.

Okay, that part wasn't so relaxing, especially given the tight constraints I had with my budget. There wasn't much wiggle room, especially not with the renovation going on next door. But I'd make it work. There really wasn't much of a choice.

It wasn't the first time I'd built something from nothing. But I did hope it would be the last.

Back in Ontario, in what felt like a different life, I had my own shop. A cozy, thriving little gift shop, Nook & Nest. Hand-poured candles, locally created art, those little adorable felt animals that no one needed but were too cute to pass up. It had taken me years to build the shop into a thriving business, and Ken had wiped it all out in months.

My ex-husband had been charming in a way that made people lean in and want to be near him. He had a way of speaking so people not only listened to everything he had to say, but they believed whatever came out of his mouth.

He was the kind of guy who could sweet-talk a vendor into giving us more credit. Credit we didn't need. And I didn't know about.

It was my shop, but I'd been naive enough to include him on the bank accounts. After all, he was my husband. I had no reason to believe he would do anything to put the shop—or us—in jeopardy.

By the time I realized he'd been *borrowing* money from the business, and we were deeply and irreversibly in debt, it was way too late.

Even as the depth of his deception came to light, he still tried to charm his way out of the situation and convince me it would all be okay. He'd been so smooth, so confident that I started to second-guess things and question my own decision. But the truth was, Ken had been so completely reckless with our livelihood that it had taken only months to destroy everything. In a flash, I lost it all.

My business, my savings, my marriage, and my peace.

So no, I didn't trust a handsome smile and a charming word. Not anymore.

It had taken me years to rebuild my credit and scrimp and save for my new shop. Plot Twist was all I had. And I'd be damned if I let the smooth-talking brewmaster next door ruin it. Not even if the way he smiled at me made something low in my belly tighten. *Especially* because of that.

I shut my laptop and exhaled slowly, forcing myself back into the present. The past didn't get to control me here. I'd moved across the country to this small mountain town where no one knew me or my past. This wasn't just my second chance—it was my *last* chance. The thought of starting over again was too exhausting to contemplate.

I carried the teacup to the sink and rinsed the rest of the brew down the drain before refilling the cup with water for my one plant, a scraggly pothos I'd named Priscilla. She'd been left in the shop by the previous owner when I'd taken over the lease, and despite her less-than-lush appearance, I couldn't bring myself to give up on her.

I glanced out the window into the busy plaza below. The pedestrian-only area of Trickle Creek, lined with shops, cafes, and bustling businesses, was one of the reasons I'd fallen in love with this town and the shop space. From here, I could see the Bean Bag across the way, the Sugar Shack that served the best ice cream and more recently, homemade chocolates and the little diner, Willa's Whisk, run by Willa herself, who had to be at least eighty. Right around the corner was Lauren's shop, and across from that, the flower shop, Alpenglow. The owner, Charli, was known for her beautiful displays that she customized for every store and changed out with the seasons.

The plaza was pedestrian-only, which was why the large flatbed truck slowly making its way through the cobblestoned street caught my attention. It was loaded down with equipment, a small forklift following behind.

The brewery.

As I watched, Ethan and two of his brothers worked together to unload what had to be a brewing tank and maneuvered it into the old Chinese food restaurant, through what used to be a large picture window but was now a gaping hole in the front of the store.

I rolled my eyes. So much for a peaceful Sunday.

A few moments later, a loud clatter echoed through the wall. I muttered a curse under my breath and was just about to turn away to ignore the construction when a thunderous crash rang out from below.

Then silence.

My stomach dropped.

That could not be good.

"No, no, no—" I hurried down the stairs two at a time and burst through the staff door at the back of my store just in time to see a puff of dust blow through the old vent cover on the wall.

I stopped dead as the fine cloud of white plaster dust drifted through the air above me and settled gently, like a thick carpet on absolutely everything.

Including me.

My cozy seating area, where the Sunday writing group was set to meet in just under two hours, was blanketed in white. The couch, the armchairs, the coffee table with the stack of writing prompt cards I'd just arranged—all coated in powder.

I blinked through the dust, not able to fully process what I was seeing.

And then, very calmly, I took a breath and said, "You have *got* to be kidding me."

Ethan

The tank slammed into the venting system with a screech and crunch of metal.

"Dammit." I swallowed back the litany of curse words I wanted to use despite the fact that Quinn wasn't there to give me trouble and force me to put money in the swear jar. "I told you we needed more clearance, Grayson."

"It's not my fault," my brother called from behind the controls of the forklift he'd borrowed from the hardware shop he managed. "Brody's the one giving directions."

"Oh no." My eldest brother held up his hands, apparently also unwilling to take ownership for the accident that had now left the ductwork dangling from the ceiling. "I was watching *this* side." He pointed toward me. "You said you had things under control from over there."

He wasn't wrong. Besides, ultimately, the responsibility started and ended with me. It was *my* brewery.

And it was my fucking mess to clean up.

I shot both of them a glare, but swallowed back my arguments. I was too damn tired for them anyway. My back ached, Quinn's math worksheet was still sitting half-finished on the kitchen table with a promise I hoped like hell I could keep to help her finish it up later, and now my brand-new tank had just caused me yet another setback.

Great start to the day. Never mind that I still needed to get two more tanks unloaded from the truck before the overhead door installers showed up on Monday morning.

The only benefit to taking out the huge picture window in the storefront, creating a massive, gaping hole, was that I could replace it with an all-glass garage door-style setup that could be opened on summer days.

But for the moment, I needed to focus on the problem at hand.

"You've got to be kidding me."

I squeezed my eyes shut and pinched the bridge of my

nose at the sound of her voice, because apparently, I now also had another problem to deal with.

I turned to see Delaney storming into the space, her arms crossed over her black sweater, now covered in fine white powder. There was a smudge of dust on her cheek, and if she weren't glaring at me like she wanted to murder me, I might've smiled.

Her cheeks were flushed, lips pressed into a tight line, and her jaw set as she jabbed a finger at me.

"Were you aware that you just vented all of *your* plaster dust into *my* store?"

I let out a breath and straightened my shoulders, feeling the knot of tension there. "Well, considering I just smashed my brand-new tank into the vents, I imagine that probably did happen."

"I have a writing group meeting in a little over an hour and everything—I mean *everything*, including me—is covered in this mess."

I didn't have time to deal with this. Not on top of everything else.

"Yeah, well, I've got tanks to install and a hole in the front of my shop to seal up, Delaney. We all have problems."

"I get that," she said through clenched teeth. "But maybe next time you could give me a heads-up before you—"

"I didn't exactly plan to hit the vent, Delaney," I said, a little sharper than I intended. "Maybe next time, you can remember that this isn't just *your* plaza. My business matters, too. This isn't just a hobby, you know. I've got my own bills to pay."

Bills that were piling up by the day. I tried not to think of it, but I *was* on a tight timeline. I needed to get things up and running as soon as possible, or we'd have to start dipping into my savings.

"I never said it was a hobby." Her eyes flared, but there was a shake in her voice that hadn't been there a moment ago.

"Could've fooled me," I muttered, turning back to the tank.

"Look, Ethan. I have to——"

"Enough, Delaney." I spun around to face her. "I'm sorry I got dust in your store, okay? But I didn't mean for that to happen. I've tried to work around your schedule as much as possible, but the fact of the matter is, I have a timeline of my own. If that means there's a little dust for a few days, you're going to have to learn to deal with it."

Her eyes widened. "A little dust?"

Okay, I could admit that came out way worse than I'd intended. But it was too late to take it back, and frankly, I didn't have the bandwidth to apologize.

She stared at me as though she couldn't decide whether she wanted to scream at me or hit me. Before she could do either, she spun on her heel and stormed out the way she came.

Brody let out a low whistle behind me. "Damn, brother. You sure know how to charm a lady."

Grayson burst out in laughter, but I didn't have the time or patience for either of them. "Shut up and help me get the other tanks in."

But even as I turned back to my work, I couldn't stop thinking about Delaney. The way her eyes flashed when she was mad. The way her tits pressed up in her bulky sweater when she crossed her arms. And of course the way she was a giant pain in my ass.

BY THE TIME we got all the tanks in position, the only thing I really wanted to do was go home and take a long shower and crawl into bed.

Unfortunately, when there was a family dinner on the schedule, that wasn't an option.

And really, an actual meal would probably be good for me.

Brody's place smelled like roasted garlic and fresh bread the moment I stepped inside what was once our childhood home. My eldest brother bought it from our mother when she decided to move south.

"It smells delicious in here," I told Avery when I entered the kitchen. Reid's wife kissed me on the cheek before turning back to the stove to stir the spaghetti sauce. There were a lot of reasons why we all loved Avery, not the least of which was the fact that her sunshiney, bubbly demeanor was a good balance for our grouchy brother. But her cooking was also a very welcome addition to our family.

No matter whose turn it was to cook, the family dinners took place at Brody's, mostly because it was tradition, but also because it would never not feel like home for all of us. Something just made us all feel good inside to gather around the old kitchen table and share a meal.

Grayson and Quinn were at the kitchen table, bent over the worksheet I'd started with her that morning. "How's the homework going, kiddo?" I tried to ruffle her hair, but she dodged my efforts.

"Uncle Gray is super smart." She gave me a pointed look and bit the end of her pencil.

"Are you saying I'm not?"

She shrugged. "I didn't say that exactly."

My brother laughed, but I only shook my head. Before Quinn was born, I had a successful career in finance in the city, but Polly's career in oil and gas took off faster than we'd planned. She was great at her job, but motherhood never suited her.

I happily scaled back my role at the office to be with Quinn, pivoting to managing our family stock portfolio in the evenings and filling my days with playdates and daddy-and-me classes.

I never missed my old corporate life, but now that Quinn was older and it was just the two of us rebuilding our lives, it was the perfect time to start something new. A new challenge and a fresh start.

"It smells amazing in here." Our youngest brother, Preston, burst through the door, looking like he'd been playing in the dirt. "Am I late?"

"What the hell happened to you?" Brody joined us in the kitchen and moved straight to the fridge to grab us some cold beer.

Still not my brews, but with the new tanks finally installed, it wouldn't be long before I had some samples.

"I hit a rock on the trail," Preston said. "I was out past Bootleg Mountain and wasn't paying attention. Took a little tumble, but nothing crazy."

Grayson and I exchanged a glance. *Nothing crazy* for Preston on his mountain bike had an entirely different meaning for almost anyone else. Still, we all knew it wasn't worth giving our brother a hard time about his daredevil behavior.

"Go wash up," Avery told him. "As soon as Quinn's done her homework, it's time to eat."

"I'm done!" On cue, Quinn held her paper in the air and waved it around. "Let's eat!"

I shook my head, but couldn't help but smile. "Help me set the table, kiddo."

A few minutes later, everyone was as cleaned up as they were going to be, the table was set, and plates were filled. Laughter filled the room the way it always did when we were together.

There was nothing better than having my family all together. It was the main reason I'd moved back to Trickle Creek. I know Quinn missed her friends in the city, but she'd find her tribe here, too. I knew she would. And in the meantime, I hoped having her uncles would help bridge the gap.

I was halfway through my second helping of Avery's spaghetti and meatballs when Reid leaned back in his chair and gave me a look. "So, I heard you weren't quite as charming to your new neighbor today. I thought I was supposed to be the grumpy one."

Avery gave him an affectionate look. She was the only one Reid wasn't a total ass to. Well, her and Quinn.

Grayson didn't even try to hide his grin. "Delaney? Oh yeah. She stormed in looking like she'd just doused herself with a bag of flour. And she was pissed."

"The vent was an accident." An accident that was going to be damn expensive.

"You did kind of snap at her, man," Brody added.

I sighed and put my fork down. "I didn't snap." Then I caught Quinn's raised brow from across the table. "Okay, maybe I was a little short with her, but it was a stressful moment and—"

"Dad! The bookstore lady is awesome. Don't be mean to her."

"I wasn't—"

"You were."

I shot Grayson a look.

"What?" he said with feigned innocence. "You were a dick."

"Don't swear in front of Quinn."

"You owe me a dollar, Uncle Gray."

Happy the heat was off me for a moment, I picked up the fork and shoved a bite of pasta in my mouth.

Grayson handed over the money to my smirking daughter. She was going to be able to afford her own car by the time she was sixteen if we didn't watch our mouths.

"You have to apologize, Dad. I like Delaney," Quinn said after a moment. "She's cool. And she lets me hang out in the corner and read whatever I want. She even lets me borrow books."

Brody nodded and grinned. "She also gives your dad a run for his money and seems to be totally immune to his charms."

"It is entertaining," Grayson added. "The way she gets under his skin."

"Stop. Talking." I pointed my fork at each of them in turn. The last thing I needed was my way-too-perceptive daughter picking up on any energy between Delaney and me that wasn't strictly neighborly.

Especially when I still wasn't sure myself what that energy was.

Well, on her end, it was pure annoyance.

"You can't blame her for being annoyed, really," Brody said. "That was *a lot* of dust."

"*Dad!*"

I blew out a sigh and pushed back from the table, my appetite suddenly gone. "Fine. I'll apologize."

"Tomorrow?" Reid asked, his eyebrows raised.

"Yes," I said with a grunt. "Tomorrow."

I really was going to have to speak to my brothers about minding their own business.

Chapter Four

Delaney

It had already been a long day. Half of my latest shipment of trade paperbacks I'd ordered had arrived damaged. My part-time girl had called in sick, and to top it all off, I was *still* finding plaster dust on every single surface in the shop.

By some miracle, I'd managed to clean the chairs and tables in my reading and meeting nook in time for the writing group to meet the day before, but the rest of the shop had taken way longer. I'd been up way later than I should have been, putting things back in order.

What I really needed was to soak in a hot bath with a glass of wine. Instead, I was getting ready to settle into a plastic folding chair for the next few hours for the town meeting.

As a business owner, it was a good idea to participate in these things, especially considering the agenda was set to discuss the upcoming Fall into the Plaza event.

The town hall smelled like old paper and lemon cleaner.

The scratch of folding chairs on the old floor mingled with the happy chatter of the townspeople as I stepped inside.

I spotted Ethan before he saw me. He stood near the back, talking next to his brother, who managed the hardware store. He looked like he was scanning the room for someone and only half listening to whatever Grayson was saying. When his gaze shifted my way, I veered to the left and slipped into an empty seat next to Lauren before he could make eye contact.

"You're avoiding him," Lauren said, not even trying to hide the fact that she was looking at Ethan over my shoulder.

"Who?" I played dumb.

She raised her eyebrow and laughed before she asked, "Did you get the mess cleaned up?"

"It took me all day." I let out a breath and picked up a copy of the agenda from the stack next to me. "And most of the night, too. Not that he'd care." I looked at my friend. "Do you know that somehow he managed to make it seem like it was my fault?"

Lauren gave me a sympathetic smile. "I'm sure the construction will be over soon."

"Right." I tried not to groan. "And then I'll only have to deal with the fact that there's an entire brewery full of people drinking next door to my peaceful little shop." I exhaled slowly and tried to clear my thoughts. "Sorry," I said to Lauren. "I don't mean to be so negative. I'm just exhausted. And I really need a break from…well, the mess." I put a smile on my face. "You're right. It will be over soon."

Lauren squeezed my arm. "I know this isn't your first choice, but maybe this meeting can be a little break from all—"

"Ladies." Brody Lyons dropped into the seat on

Lauren's other side with a flash of that smile that made him one of the most well-liked people in Trickle Creek.

The same charming smile his brother had.

I pushed the thought from my mind. Ethan's type of charm was different. Brody was warm, affable, and easy to like. Plus, he wasn't the brother whose construction zone was currently threatening my livelihood.

He and Lauren bumped elbows and exchanged a quiet laugh. The way they moved around each other always made me wonder why they weren't together. We hadn't known each other long enough for me to be comfortable asking Lauren about it, but their chemistry was obvious.

I didn't have much time to ponder it, though, because a moment later, the seat on *my* other side scraped back. I turned as Ethan settled his big frame into the chair next to me.

My shoulders stiffened reflexively. I turned away, but not before I saw his easy smile. He smelled of soap and sawdust and whatever sinfully good cologne he was wearing that should be outlawed in a small, enclosed space where I had to sit next to him.

I didn't acknowledge him.

"Evening," he said anyway, low and smooth, just loud enough for me to hear. "I was hoping you—"

"Of course I was going to be here." I cut him off sharply. "My business is important to me."

"I think we've established that already."

I turned and glared at him for a second before straightening my shoulders again, focusing on the front of the room.

"The agenda looks like—"

"The meeting is starting," I said, grateful for the distraction.

Next to me, I could have sworn I heard Lauren and Brody giggle. I regretted my choice of seat, but it was too late to change without looking stupid, so I focused on the council at the front of the room as the meeting started with the usual budget updates and long-winded acknowledgments on the progress of various committees.

Finally, the focus shifted to the only reason I'd attended. At the front of the room, Tilley Beckett moved in front of the crowd. Tilley was the head of the festival committee—yes, Trickle Creek had a festival committee chair. The town took their celebrations very seriously.

Tilley, who, from everything I'd been told, had held the position both officially and unofficially as long as anyone could remember, stood and clapped her hands for attention.

"Okay," she started. "Fall into the Plaza is just over a week away. There are still a few details to work out."

A few murmurs rippled through the room. I didn't miss Lauren's quiet groan beside me.

"This year," Tilley continued, "we'll be doing the passport challenge again. Any business that wants to participate will give customers a stamp on their *leaf.*" Tilley held up a big construction paper maple leaf. "Once the card is full, they can enter for a raffle prize basket. Prizes donated by all of you, of course."

Someone asked a question about booth sizes, and another about permits. I was halfway checking off my mental to-do list when Ethan's voice broke through.

"Sorry to interrupt," he said. "But I don't have a booth."

My attention snapped back to the meeting as Tilley slid her glasses up her nose and assessed Ethan. "That's right," she said. "We set up the map of the tables before you took over the space with your new brewery."

Next to me, Ethan nodded. "I was just wondering if there are extras or any way to squeeze one in."

"Hmm." Tilley looked concerned. "The maps, information flyers, and posters have already been printed up, Ethan. I'm not sure what we can do."

Someone on the other side of the room spoke up. "Maybe another business could share?"

Instinctively, I stiffened. I knew exactly what was coming before anyone said it out loud. The universe was lining up to screw with me.

I dropped my gaze to my lap, but there was nowhere to hide.

"Delaney."

I flinched at the sound of my name on Tilley's lips.

"You're right next door, and you have a great spot with excellent visibility. What do you think?"

Every eye in the room turned to me. Including his.

I could feel Ethan's gaze burning into me. Hot. Expectant. And I'm sure there was a grin on his lips, too. I didn't need to confirm it by looking.

"I...I..." I cleared my throat. "Sure. Fine."

"Perfect." Tilley beamed. "I'm sure it'll be a match made in heaven."

I definitely wasn't sure about that. But it's not like I had much of a choice.

"This will be fun."

I didn't look at him. But I knew he was smiling. I could hear it in his voice. And damn it if my stupid heart didn't have the nerve to flutter in response.

· · ·

Ethan

"Delaney."

I reached for her, but the moment the meeting was adjourned, she jumped up and was halfway down the aisle to the door before I managed to extract myself from the tiny chair and go after her.

I wasn't going to let her walk away like this without at least trying to apologize. After all, I had promised Quinn. But even if I hadn't, now we were going to be working together and…

"Hey." I managed to intercept her as she reached the door. "Delaney." I tried to keep my tone casual but for some reason, my heart was pounding. Grayson was right; something about this woman got under my skin. "Can we talk for a minute?"

She stopped, and her shoulders stiffened. She didn't look at me. I could see the tension in the set of her back, but at least she didn't walk off right away. It wasn't much, but I'd take it.

After a moment, she blew out an exasperated breath and turned to look at me.

"I'm sorry for yesterday." My words came out a bit quicker than I'd meant. "I was…it was a bad day. Stress got the better of me, and I snapped at you. I'm sorry. I shouldn't have been so short. You didn't deserve that."

Her expression softened, so I pressed on. "It looks like we're going to be working together for the festival. Thank you for sharing a table with me. It means a lot that you—"

"I didn't really have a choice, did I?"

Her words were sharp, but I wasn't going to be deterred.

"Regardless, I appreciate it." I flashed her a smile, but she still didn't crack. "Maybe we should try to start fresh.

How about we grab a coffee later this week? We can go over our plans for the booth and see how we can work it all out together."

She was a tough nut to crack. Maybe I'd pushed her further than I'd thought. There was a slight hesitation before she responded. I held my breath, half expecting her to shoot me down again.

Finally, her lips parted. "Okay. Coffee," she said. "But you're paying."

I couldn't help the smile that tugged at the corner of my mouth. It wasn't much, but I'd take whatever crack in her exterior I could get.

"Deal," I said. "Tomorrow?"

"Two o'clock. Let's get this over with." She turned quickly to leave, but before she slipped out the front door, I caught the faintest trace of a smile on her lips.

Maybe this would work out after all.

Chapter Five

Ethan

The tanks were in. Wired, plumbed, and humming and ready to work.

The last few days had been a whirlwind, but it had been worth it. For the first time in weeks, I let myself breathe.

The venting had been fixed. The big garage door window had been successfully installed. And after what felt like forever, the smell of grease in the old walls had been replaced with the scent of fresh paint and sawdust.

More and more, the space was starting to feel like a real brewery, rather than an old Chinese food restaurant.

My brewery.

I stood in the middle of the room and let myself enjoy the quiet moment.

Well, it wasn't entirely quiet. Somewhere in the back, I could hear hammering and the sound of a truck backing up with the delivery of the bar tops that Reid had handcrafted. It was still chaotic. But at least it felt a little more like controlled chaos.

Things were coming together.

Finally.

I was itching to get started by mixing up my first brew in the new tanks instead of the little ones I'd been using in my backyard shed. I'd been playing around and refining things for months. Tweaking until I got the ratios of water, malt, and hops just right. The first brew in the tanks would be a milestone. And would be the first batch I'd have on tap in Peaks & Brews. But it would have to wait.

I checked the time on my phone and cursed under my breath. I was already late for my meeting with Delaney. The last thing I needed was to give her another reason to write me off.

I finally felt like I might have made a little headway with her the night before. Well, maybe not too much headway, but at least she hadn't yelled at me.

I grabbed my flannel from where it was hanging on a ladder and jogged across the plaza toward the coffee shop. The sun was out, but there was an unmistakable crispness in the air that meant fall had officially taken root.

Autumn in the mountains could be interesting. There were still plenty of warm days, mixed in with the cooler nights, but at any time, we could be hit with an early snowstorm. You never knew what was coming next.

I pushed open the door of the Bean Bag, the rich scent of espresso and cinnamon greeting me with a warm blast.

I took a moment to inhale the deliciousness before scanning the small room.

Her head was bent over a notebook. She was furiously scribbling notes. She didn't see me right away, so I took a moment to watch her and let my heart rate come down. I'd like to tell myself it was from the quick jog over here, but there was something undeniable about Delaney Hart that, despite every reason not to, made my heart race like a teenage boy's.

Delaney already had a coffee in front of her, so I ordered one for myself and an extra-large cookie that I hoped she'd share with me and made my way to the table.

"Sorry I'm late."

She lifted her head at the sound of my voice. For the flash of a second, before she schooled her features into her mask of distaste, I saw the softness there.

"You're late."

"I just said sorry." I set the cookie down between us. "I got a peace offering."

Her lips twitched—just barely—but I didn't miss it.

She glanced at the plate. "Oatmeal chocolate chip?"

"The best kind." I slid into the chair across from her. "It's like a granola bar and a chocolate bar had a baby."

Despite herself, half a laugh escaped her lips. "That's a disturbing image."

"Maybe." I winked. "But not inaccurate."

"No." She shook her head, but the smile stayed on her face. "I guess you're right."

I still had a long way to go with her, but at least she was no longer openly hostile toward me. I'd take whatever win I could get.

I broke the cookie in half and pushed the plate toward her.

Delaney hesitated a second before she picked it up. "Oatmeal chocolate chip is my favorite."

"Really?" I was genuinely surprised. "Mine too."

Her eyes widened. "That's not true."

"It is." I broke a piece off and popped it into my mouth. "But you need to be careful because some people like to sneak raisins into their oatmeal cookies."

"Monsters!"

"I agree." I tried not to smile as I took another bite.

"Fruit—especially raisins—has no place in baked goods." She broke off her own piece of cookie; her eyes fluttered closed momentarily as she enjoyed the burst of sugar in her mouth.

It was a sight that did something to me. Something I had no business feeling.

I cleared my throat and glanced away. "What about apple pie?"

"It's a rare exception," she said seriously. "But give me a cinnamon coffee cake or vanilla scone any day over something with fruit in it."

Interesting. It was a detail I filed away in the back of my mind.

I nodded my head toward her notebook. "Working on a few ideas for the big day?"

She blushed and shrugged, suddenly shy.

The shifts in her personality were fascinating. Now that she'd let her guard down a little and wasn't yelling at me for making too much noise or mess, Delaney seemed softer. More approachable. Kind of sweet even.

I wouldn't deny that I enjoyed her feisty side, but I liked this version of her, too.

Hell, maybe I just liked Delaney.

"I actually have a few ideas," she said after a moment. "But...I think I just thought of something better."

"Better?" I leaned in, intrigued.

"What if we did beer pairings with genres?"

"Genres?"

"Like an IPA with thriller. A sour with horror. A wheat ale with romance. That kind of thing. Match the flavor profiles with the feel of the books."

"You know your beers."

She shrugged. "Did you think I wouldn't?"

Truthfully, I'd pegged her more for a rosé or chardonnay kind of lady, but I didn't bother saying it out loud. Instead, I focused on what was truly a brilliant idea.

"That's actually…genius," I said truthfully. "Maybe a dark stout with a historical saga. Or a cozy mystery with something kind of spiced…" My mind drifted to the few brews I currently had back in my shed and mentally calculated what I could get done in time.

"You know your books." She crossed her arms and smiled, her turn to be surprised.

"You didn't think I would?"

"I guess, I…" She laughed and went with the truth. "No," she admitted. "I didn't peg you for much of a reader."

If I were being entirely honest, it had been a while since I'd had time to sit down with a novel and read for fun. But it didn't mean I didn't like it. "When I have the time, I'm a science fiction fan."

"*Wheel of Time* or *Game of Thrones*?"

"I have to pick one?"

She nodded.

"*Wheel of Time*. Easy."

The smile that slowly crossed her lips and lit up her face was the first warm, genuine one I'd seen from her. The fact that something I'd said had brought it out of her filled me with pleasure.

"I think this could be a pretty good partnership, Delaney."

She tilted her head. "I'm still not entirely convinced."

"Ouch."

"But," she broke off another piece of cookie, "I'm starting to think it might not be a total disaster."

I picked up the last piece of my half and raised it to her. "I'll cheers to that."

She laughed as crumbs fell to the table after our cookie toast. She still had her guard up, but something had shifted. And I was happy to take whatever opening I could get.

Delaney

The shop was blissfully quiet. Two customers browsed in the back, their soft murmurs floating to my ears occasionally while they discussed new finds with each other.

Dust motes danced in the sunlight, but for the first time in days, the dust wasn't coming from the construction mess from next door.

The meeting with Ethan had gone better than I'd expected. To be fair, I wasn't expecting much. But I was definitely not expecting him to offer up an oatmeal chocolate chip cookie—my favorite—and his too, apparently.

I smiled with the memory of the way we'd bonded, even momentarily, about our mutual dislike of fruit in baked goods. I couldn't remember the last time I'd met someone else who didn't think that was sacrilegious.

That one tiny moment had cracked something in me. Not much. But just enough to let in the smallest sliver of something that felt a little too close to charm.

Ethan is not Ken.

I needed to keep reminding myself of that. They weren't the same.

Ethan was a bit more rugged. Just a little rough around the edges. But there was something about him that was polished, too. Like maybe he was once a businessman instead of a brewmaster.

The reality was, I didn't know much about my next-door neighbor at all.

Except that he had a very disarming smile and a way of getting me to drop my guard.

It was dangerous.

I blew out a sigh and wandered toward the counter where I'd begun pulling books for our pairing idea. The concept had come out of nowhere, but as soon as we'd started discussing it, I couldn't stop thinking about it. As soon as I'd returned, I'd started putting together my selections.

A romance. A cozy mystery...

The fantasy section drew me in. I reached for the familiar title—*The Eye of the World*—smiling to myself.

Ethan's favorite.

I had to admit, it had surprised me that he was a reader. I hadn't expected his eyes to light up the way they had when he told me that *Wheel of Time* was his favorite series.

The bell over the door jingled. I turned to see Quinn. Her backpack was slung over her shoulder, her hair tousled, and her cheeks pinked from the crisp breeze outside.

"Hey, bookstore lady."

I smiled at her nickname for me. "School out already?"

"Thankfully." The girl dropped herself dramatically into the overstuffed chair in the reading nook. "I don't think I could handle any more math today. Especially now that I know there's a book two." She produced the dog-eared paperback I'd lent her from the depths of her pack and tossed it on the low table.

"You're done already?"

"I stayed up late," she admitted. "I had to know what

happened." She looked up at me with such excitement in her eyes, I had to laugh.

I knew she'd be ready for book two. I already had it tucked away for her.

"I hope you're still getting enough sleep." I handed her the sequel. "I don't want your parents coming in here giving me a hard time for contributing to your exhaustion. Sleep is important for school."

She rolled her eyes and groaned, "Now, you're starting to sound like my dad." She lifted her hand, mimicking a talking motion. "Sleep is important, blah blah blah. Don't stay up all night, blah blah blah."

"It sounds like he knows what he's talking about." But I hid my face so she couldn't see me smile. Quinn was so much like I was at that age. Sneaking a flashlight into my room so I could read under the covers long after I should have been asleep.

"Oh, *The Eye of the World*," Quinn said, noticing the book in my hand.

"You've read it?" I raised my brow.

"Nope." She shook her head. "I don't think it's really my style." She shrugged and flopped back, throwing her legs over the arm of the chair as she flipped the cover of the new book open. "But it's my dad's favorite."

Something clicked in my brain. I looked down at the book and back at Quinn. "Your dad?"

"Yup." She didn't look up, already absorbed in her new read. "He rereads the whole series sometimes. Like from the very beginning."

"He does what?"

With a sigh, Quinn lowered her book. "I know, right? It's intense. Those are massive books, and there are so many of them."

She wasn't wrong.

"Only, I haven't seen those books since we moved. He probably hasn't even unpacked them yet, he's been so busy."

I swallowed hard and lowered the book. "What about your mom?" I'd never directly asked Quinn about her parents. It didn't seem my place, but now…

Her eyes clouded and her jaw flexed. "My mom's even busier. But she doesn't live with us. When they got divorced, she stayed in the city 'cause of work. All my friends are there, too. But Dad wanted me to be closer to my uncles." She shrugged and the tension seemed to relax. "And they're cool."

Uncles. Single dad. Busy.

It all made sense. I can't believe I didn't see it before.

"Your dad," I said slowly, "his name is Ethan?"

"Yeah." She looked at me as if I'd just grown an arm out of my head. "You didn't know that? He's your neighbor." She waved toward our shared wall.

"Well, I knew that Ethan was my neighbor." *Did I ever.* "But I didn't know he was your dad."

Quinn offered up a shrug, already lost in her new book.

I stood there as all the pieces slid into place.

And I still had so many questions.

Mainly, how had I *not* known?

There might be more to this man who'd somehow charmed his way into driving me crazy.

And I wasn't sure what was more dangerous—that, or the way I couldn't help myself from wanting to know more.

Chapter Six

Ethan

"Quinn! You alive in there?" I tossed a blanket over the back of the couch and peeked down the hallway but there was still no sign of her.

"Almost done!" Quinn called from her bedroom.

Almost done likely meant she'd stuffed everything under her bed and called her room *clean.*

I smiled to myself, knowing I wouldn't do anything to press the issue. I'd learned to pick my battles when it came to parenting, and an immaculate room was not a battle I was willing to go to war over.

I tossed a throw pillow aside and grabbed the remote to queue up the streaming app and my movie selection. It was my night to pick the movie, which meant Quinn would roll her eyes, mumble something about how old I was, and then get way too invested by the twenty-minute mark.

Besides, I knew she'd love my latest selection.

She finally padded into the living room wearing bright-green fuzzy socks and a hoodie that was at least three sizes too big—one she'd stolen from her Uncle Brody's closet. I shook my head. As the only kid in the family, she had every single one of us wrapped around her little finger.

Her hair was piled on top of her head in some sort of messy knot, and she was already munching on something loud and aggressively neon-orange colored.

"Okay." She flopped down next to me. "I got the snacks. Movie night rules."

I peered into the bowl and shook my head. "That doesn't look like food."

"They're delicious." She held an orange thing out at me before biting into it with a grin. "What oldie are you torturing me with tonight?"

She grinned because we both knew how much we loved our little tradition. I'd started it when she was young and the two of us found ourselves alone on Saturday nights while her mother was wining and dining clients or away at conferences or whatever else Polly was out doing that was more important than her family.

When she was little, Quinn would choose the latest Disney film to hit the streaming services, while I chose the cartoon classics from my youth.

As she got older, so did our selections. It had become a fun game to see what the other would come up with.

We'd been so busy since moving back to Trickle Creek, but I always made time for Quinn and our special moments together.

"You're going to love it," I told her. "It's a classic."

Quinn groaned. "Classic is code for *old*." She dragged the word out, and I laughed as I queued up *The Breakfast Club*.

"Are those gummy bears in there, too?" I gave her the

side eye as she dug into the bowl and tossed a little bear into her mouth.

"Delaney said they're movie night must-haves."

Something in my gut tightened at the mention of my bookshop neighbor. "Did she?" I tried to sound casual, but Quinn must have noticed something in my voice, judging by the sidelong glance she gave me.

"Yeah. Right before she told me she was going out tonight."

"Oh?" Once again, I struggled to sound neutral when I felt nothing of the sort at the thought of Delaney out with some guy. "A date?"

"Nice, Dad." My daughter laughed and stuffed a strange mixture of bright-orange cheese snacks and gummy bears into her mouth.

"What? I can be curious."

"You're being nosy," she informed me. "But no, she's out with the girls. Trivia night at the Wildflower. Whatever that is."

Interesting.

I tried not to look like I cared, but I wasn't hiding it well.

"She said she doesn't even like trivia night. Apparently, it's all about the wine and the meat."

I almost spat out my soda. "The *meat?*"

Quinn shrugged. "Meat and cheese and grapes or something. Some kinda board."

I couldn't help but laugh. "A charcuterie board?"

"Whatever."

I hit play on the movie, but I was too distracted to pay any attention to the opening scene. All I could picture was Delaney sitting at one of the high-top tables, laughing with her friends. Was she dressed up? Or wearing the big, knitted cardigan she always seemed to have on over those tight Tshirts that made it increasingly harder to keep my thoughts friendly?

Which meant, other men probably thought the same thing. For some reason, the idea of any other man looking at Delaney the way I looked at her stirred up something suspiciously close to jealousy deep inside.

"So, wait, they're all in detention?" Quinn's question jarred me from my thoughts.

"What?"

"The movie, Dad." She jabbed a finger toward the screen. "They're in detention? On a Saturday?"

"Oh. Right."

I took a breath, pushed the thoughts of Delaney aside, and focused on the movie and my daughter, reminding myself that the best part of my night was already sitting right next to me.

Delaney

"How did you not know that one?" Kat stared at me as if it were my fault we were currently in last place for trivia night.

Sure, I *should* have been able to answer the last question, but we sucked as a group. It took a real team effort to do as badly as we were doing.

I was starting to regret accepting Lauren's invite to trivia night. I told her I was no good at trivia, but she promised me an amazing charcuterie board, which it was. Besides, it was long past time I got to know some more people.

"I mean, you *do* own a bookstore." Lauren shot me a look. "How did you not know who wrote *The Handmaid's Tale?*"

"I know it's Margaret Atwood." I reached for a cracker and put a dollop of fig jam on top. "I did warn you that I 'm not good at this. I blank when the question is asked." I popped the cracker in my mouth.

Lauren laughed because she knew it was true. "If they asked what color the sky was, I think she'd still get it wrong."

"Exactly." I reached for a grape. "I don't know why I am the way I am. But I am totally useless at this."

"Lucky for you," Avery chimed in, "it's not about getting the questions right." The woman smiled in my direction. "It's about the snacks."

"I couldn't agree more." I grinned as I stacked a piece of peppered salami with a slab of brie. "And I do appreciate the invitation. Despite the fact that I'm not a lot of help."

"We're happy to have you," Kat said. "I'm just happy to get out of the house for a few hours."

I'd run into Kat a few times since we both owned businesses in the plaza. Kat Carlson, soon to be Kat Fisher, ran the hair salon in town, Strands, and had lived in Trickle Creek her entire life. She was the youngest daughter of the town savior, Michael Carlson, who passed away a few years ago after being credited for single-handedly saving the town by bringing in more tourism after the mining industry closed.

She was also a new mother of a baby boy, and cherished her rare nights out.

Avery Walker was even newer to town than I was, having moved back recently after inheriting the Tamarack Inn. She'd married Reid Lyons, Ethan's brother, in order to keep her inheritance. In a town the size of Trickle Creek, everyone seemed to be connected in some way.

I was thankful for the opportunity to get to know them better. Especially considering they were both warm, friendly, and incredibly easy to talk to.

"I hear you're working with Ethan on the Fall into the Plaza event."

The change of subject was so abrupt, I almost choked on the candied almond I'd been chewing.

"I was sorry to miss the meeting the other day, but I heard Tilley didn't give you much of a choice," Avery added.

"She sure didn't." I shook my head.

"Not that it's too much of an imposition to work with a sexy brewmaster, though, is it, Delaney?"

I shot a glare toward my best friend, but Lauren either didn't seem to notice or didn't care. She grinned back at me.

"I don't know about sexy." It was a full-on lie.

"Yeah, right." Kat pretended to fan herself. "Ethan has always been a sexy beast. Even when we were kids."

"Kat!"

"What?" The redhead feigned innocence. "Just because I have Andy, who, I might add, is the hottest man in this town, especially when he holds baby Billy."

"Aww," Lauren said. "That is so sweet."

"It is," Kat agreed. "But to the point." She looked at me again. "It doesn't mean I can't appreciate a good-looking man when I see him."

I sat back in my chair and lifted my glass of pinot noir. If we didn't change topics soon, I was definitely going to need another glass.

"He is pretty hot, don't you think, Delaney?"

There was no way I was answering that. Especially considering I hadn't been able to stop thinking about Ethan and exactly how hot I thought he was, or how in recent days I'd become a lot less annoyed by him and had actually looked forward to bumping into him, or the quick exchanges we'd shared for planning the Books and Brews table we'd be hosting together in a few days.

"He's not nearly as annoying as I used to think he was," I said instead.

Kat laughed so loudly, the woman hosting trivia night shot us a dirty look. Clearly, our own efforts to win had been abandoned in favor of gossip.

"Ethan's actually a great guy," Avery said. "And an awesome dad."

My smile was genuine. "Quinn is a great kid. She spends a lot of time in Plot Twist."

"That's what I hear. Reid told me she couldn't stop talking about you and the books you've been lending her at their last ice cream date."

That made me smile. "I really enjoy her."

"What about her dad?" Kat asked with a cheeky grin. "Do you enjoy him, too? He's very charming."

"Ha." I reached for more snacks. "He definitely is that."

"You say that like it's a problem." Avery tilted her head in my direction.

I took my time chewing my snack before responding. It didn't seem like the ladies were going to let this go. "It is," I said after a moment. "The thing is, I don't go in for that charming-and-knows-it kind of thing. Nothing good can come from a charmer."

Lauren gave me a knowing nod. I hadn't told her much of my history, but she knew enough.

"What do you go in for?" Kat grabbed a cracker from the plate. "I know we don't know each other very well yet, but I don't think I've heard about you dating since you moved to town."

"Because I haven't," I said simply. "I've been there, done that. The whole long-term relationship and even marriage thing. Fool me once…" I shrugged before continuing. "I don't feel the need to lose myself in some man, only to have my heart and my whole life smashed to pieces. No thanks."

Kat let out a low whistle.

Avery grimaced. "Wow," Avery said. "That's actually kind of a cynical way to look at things."

"Not cynical." I drained the rest of my wine. "Just realistic. The shop is my focus right now. It's more than enough. I like my life fine just the way it is, thank you."

Lauren nudged me gently. "No one's saying your life isn't fine, Delaney. But it's okay to be interested. Just because you had a bad experience doesn't mean you should never trust again."

I didn't respond, and for a beat, no one pushed.

And then Kat said, "And who said anything about a relationship? Get that man into bed."

"Kat!"

"What?" She held up her hands. "No woman should live without a healthy dose of orgasms. I bet Ethan could—"

"Kat!" Avery cried again. "That's my brother-in-law you're talking about."

She shrugged. "Just calling it like I see it." She winked at me, and I laughed.

"You know, Delaney," Avery said, ignoring Kat, "Ethan's not a bad guy. I know he seems like a smooth-talking charmer, but I promise, he's not like that. He's solid. He's had to be."

Avery's comment settled into the space between us. I actually couldn't disagree with her. Ethan *had* been showing up, at least when it came to our Books and Brews event. He was treating it seriously when I'd been worried he wouldn't.

Even I had to admit that ever since our shared cookie, he'd been different toward me.

Or maybe it was *me* who had been different toward him.
Either way, something had shifted between us.
Something I was trying very hard to ignore.

"I don't know if you all have a future as matchmakers."
I forced a lightness into my voice. "But I sure do appreciate
your commitment to meddling."

They all laughed again, the mood once more changed,
and I let myself smile a little too, ignoring the little voice in
the back of my head that wondered what it might be like to
put myself out there again.

The girls kept laughing as a new round of trivia started.
Finally, the attention moved away from me and my love life.
But I let myself drift for a bit.

Could I do it? Could I let someone in again?

What if this was different? What if *Ethan* was different?

Chapter Seven

Ethan

The sky was a clear, cloudless blue, but the air was just cool enough for a sweater. The perfect day for Fall into the Plaza. And I wasn't the only one who thought so. The plaza was packed. It looked as if the entire town, and a healthy dose of tourists, had come out for the event.

Our little corner of the plaza and our Books and Brews table had enjoyed a steady flow of visitors all day and was definitely one of the more popular tables. Not that it was a competition, but I couldn't help but notice Delaney and I had way more visitors than Brody's table.

Of course, my brother wasn't offering free beer samples.

Still, I couldn't help but feel a little bit proud of our efforts.

Okay, a lot proud.

The spinning wheel I'd built from leftover plywood scraps and had Quinn paint bright colors stood tall behind the table, its wooden pointer clicking with every spin. The oohing and aahing from onlookers every time the wheel stopped on a new genre and beer pairing had been a big part of the draw at our table.

It was a total hit.

"Historical romance and a brown ale," I called out as the wheel clicked on the bright-blue wedge. "A classic pairing."

Delaney laughed and handed the woman a sample of the beer before directing her to the pile of appropriate books she'd gathered.

"Are you sure you haven't rigged the wheel?" She smiled at me after the customer moved on with her list of recommended books in hand. "I think I've handed out more romance titles than anything else today."

I grinned. "What can I say? Maybe I'm a sucker for a happily ever after."

She laughed. Soft and real, and damn if the sound didn't go straight to my chest. Delaney looked good today. *Really* good. Her burgundy scarf brought out the pink in her cheeks from the chill in the air. Her hair was down and curled naturally around her face in a slightly wild, effortless way.

I'd caught myself looking more than I should. But I couldn't help it; she was mesmerizing in a way I didn't expect and had no idea what to do with.

"I thought you were more of a sci-fi, fantasy type?" She reached over and spun the wheel absentmindedly.

"I can be two things."

She laughed again as the wheel landed on a science fiction and pale ale pairing. We both laughed easily. "What are the odds?"

"I can recommend a few selections for you." I moved casually to the stack and pulled the first in the *Wheel of Time* series. I couldn't help but notice she'd chosen my favorite for the table.

"You don't think I've read it?"

I narrowed my eyes and pretended to assess her. "I'm not sure," I said honestly. "You don't really strike me as the type who's into epic fantasy."

"Neither do you."

"Fair point."

"But I'm happy to try the beer." She winked at me and poured herself a small sample. "Honestly," Delaney said after taking a sip. "This wheel was a really good idea. I can't believe how busy we've been today. This is nuts."

"Are you saying that working with me was actually a good idea?" I wiggled my eyebrows, and she rolled her eyes.

"I'm just saying it hasn't been as bad as I expected."

"High praise." My laughter was cut short by the arrival of a new customer at our table.

An outdoorsy-type man in his thirties, wearing a fleece vest and an easy grin that was aimed directly at Delaney. He had that casual, rugged charm that guys like him always seemed to wear like a second skin, and women seemed to find attractive.

"What do you recommend?" he asked her, not even glancing in my direction.

Delaney turned her attention to the man, and I instantly missed having her focus on me. "A book or a brew?" She smiled politely.

"Spin the wheel." I motioned toward it, but he didn't bother to take his gaze off Delaney.

"Actually, I think I know exactly what I'd like," he said to Delaney, keeping his eyes locked on her.

I didn't like it. I didn't like him.

There was no logical reason for the flare of jealousy,

but logic didn't stand a chance against the green monster clawing up the back of my throat. Not that there was much I could do about it. Not without looking like a total jackass.

So I swallowed it down and focused on the couple approaching the table.

"Hey there," I said, my voice tighter than I meant it to be. "Care to spin the wheel for a pairing?"

While they moved for the wheel, snippets of Delaney's conversation reached my ears.

"I'm looking for something to take on a hike," the guy said. "Something adventurous…and maybe someone to read it with me."

Seriously?

Reluctantly, I turned back to my task, pouring a sample of the pilsner for the couple in front of me, but my hand wasn't as steady as usual. Beer sloshed over the cup and onto the table, narrowly missing a stack of books. I muttered a curse and reached for a paper towel.

I caught Delaney's response as I blotted up the mess. "I'm not much for the outdoors," she said. "But I'm sure you'll have a good time."

The guy either didn't notice or care.

I looked over in time to see Delaney hand him a book with a small, practiced smile that I noticed didn't reach her eyes.

He finally moved on, and I exhaled. Delaney turned back to the table and raised her eyebrows at the mess I'd made.

"Everything okay over here, Ethan?"

"Why wouldn't it be?"

She smirked.

"Was that true?" I asked before I could stop myself.

"About you not liking the outdoors?" I'm not sure why it mattered so much, but I needed to know.

"Not at all." Her eyes locked on mine. "I just didn't want to encourage him."

I blew out a breath. "Good."

"Good?" She looked at me pointedly, but before I could say anything, Delaney added, "Jealousy doesn't suit you."

"Wasn't jealous," I answered too quickly. "I just didn't like the way he was looking at you like it was speed dating instead of a book table."

Delaney shrugged and tossed her hair over her shoulder. "Maybe it wouldn't be the worst thing if someone did ask me out."

The words hit me square in the chest. I swallowed and forced a smile. "I mean…yeah. Makes sense, I guess," I said, aiming for casual but missing it by a mile.

She turned to help the next person, and I focused on refilling the beer samples. I managed not to spill again, but my mind was still stuck on what she'd said. Of course she deserved to be asked out on a date. Smart, sharp, funny, and gorgeous, she also managed to make running a bookstore look like the coolest job in town.

If things were different…if I wasn't already in over my head with the brewery and raising Quinn…maybe I would have said something or asked her to dinner. On a real date.

But that's not where we were. We'd come too far in our effort to make peace with each other. Even if I did have a spare minute to consider a date, I couldn't afford screwing things up with Delaney.

Instead, I focused on the next pour and pretended I didn't care who might ask her out next.

Even if I really, really did.

Delaney

By the time the sun dipped behind the mountains and the air grew chilly, my feet ached and my cheeks hurt from smiling and laughing all day. It had been a very successful event.

I stacked up the leftover books and placed them in a crate. The goal hadn't been to sell books, but to drive interest in the store. In the end, we'd done both. Plus quite a bit of enthusiasm for Ethan's brewery, set for a grand opening soon.

Ethan crouched to unlatch the legs of the spinning wheel he'd constructed, now slightly wobbly after hours of use. "I think it's safe to say this was a huge hit."

I glanced at the empty sample cups piled up in the trash bin and the handful of flyers we had left and nodded. "Okay, I have to admit. You were right about the wheel."

His grin lit up his face. "I knew you liked it."

"I told you earlier I liked it." I tilted my head and gave him a look.

"Maybe," he admitted. "But I don't think I'll ever get sick of hearing it."

Before I could fire back, a familiar voice called out. "Dad! Can I borrow twenty bucks?"

Quinn jogged toward us, her hair in her signature messy braid and a smile on her face. She slid to a stop beside the table with another girl the same age right behind her. "Hi, bookstore lady." Quinn flashed me a grin before turning back to her dad.

"Hi to you, too, kiddo." Ethan grinned. "Where've you been all day?"

"Everywhere. Did you know that over at the flower shop, you could make your own arrangement?"

"I didn't know that." Ethan stopped what he was doing to give his daughter his full attention.

"And the Sugar Shack had fudge samples."

"And I suppose you tried them all."

Quinn laughed. "But not the rum raisin, whatever that is. It sounds gross."

I did my best to swallow my giggle.

"So, can I?"

"Can you what?" Ethan asked.

"Can I borrow twenty bucks?"

"By *borrow*," he smiled, "how exactly do you plan to pay me back?"

Quinn cocked her hip and tilted her head with the attitude of a girl much older than she was. Again, I swallowed a laugh. Quinn was a great kid, but I could easily see what a handful she was going to be in a few years.

"Yes," Ethan said before she could ask again. "You can *have* twenty dollars." He reached into his back pocket and pulled his wallet out. "I assume it's not to buy fudge?"

"Nope." Quinn snatched the bill from her dad. "We want some of those giant cinnamon buns they have at the end of the plaza. They're like the size of my head."

I watched their easy back-and-forth. The warmth and love between them radiated openly. Something about seeing Ethan as a dad, so relaxed and a little goofy, so easily in sync with his daughter caught me off guard.

"Try not to have too much sugar." He raised his eyebrows. "And back here by six, okay?"

"You're the best." Quinn turned to leave with her friend, but hesitated for a moment. "Love you, Dad. Bye, bookstore lady."

"Her name is Delaney," Ethan called after her.

"I know." Quinn laughed. "It's our thing."

I didn't bother hiding my smile as Quinn and her friend took off, running in the direction of the huge cinnamon buns.

"It's your thing?" he asked with a grin.

"I guess it is." I shrugged, trying to look casual about it, but on the inside, I loved that Quinn and I had *our thing*.

"She's a handful." Ethan shook his head and blew out a breath, but his voice was filled with nothing but pride.

"She's incredible," I said softly. And then, before I could stop myself, "You're really good with her."

Ethan looked over at me, surprise on his face for half a second before his expression settled into something else. "Thanks. I'm really just figuring it out as I go."

"Well, you make it look easier than it probably is." I meant it.

He gave a little laugh and rubbed the back of his neck. "Some days feel like a win. Others...well, not so much."

I flashed him a sympathetic smile. I couldn't imagine trying to raise a twelve-year-old girl. Let alone doing it on my own.

"She's a good kid," Ethan continued. "That makes it easier."

I nodded and reached across the table to gather up the leftover flyers. The moment was over, but the warmth of watching the two of them together lingered, leaving behind the slightest ache in my chest that I didn't know what to do with.

They had an effortless rhythm together. The father-daughter connection was different, certainly, but standing on the outside of it made me realize just how long it had been since I'd felt that kind of connection with anyone.

And maybe, how much I'd missed it.

Chapter Eight

Delaney

I had a post-festival hangover. The Fall into the Plaza event had been a complete success, but spending an entire day outside on my feet *peopling* all day had taken its toll. Sure, I did a good job with my customers, and I enjoyed the relationships I made with each and every one of them. But I was an introvert at heart, and I was exhausted from the effort of being *on* all day.

All I wanted to do was hide under my comforter with a mug of tea and a good book and take a personal day.

Not an option when you ran your own business, so somehow I mustered up some energy and got myself down to the shop. Perhaps I wasn't the only one with a festival hangover, because the shop stayed mercifully quiet for most of the day.

It was late in the day and I was in the back room trying to wrestle a box of new arrivals onto the bottom shelf, when I heard the bells over the front door chime with a new customer, followed by a familiar voice.

"Bookstore lady?"

A warm smile crossed my face reflexively. "I'll be right there," I called, brushing my hands on my jeans as I stood and stretched the kink out of my back.

I stepped into the main shop, expecting to see Quinn full of life, bouncing on her toes, eager to tell me all about the book she most certainly had just finished. Instead, Quinn stood with her back to me, her shoulders hunched under her school backpack, her eyes downcast so I could tell she wasn't really scanning the shelf in front of her. Her usual bounce was noticeably absent.

"Hey, kiddo," I said, softening my voice. "How was school?"

She shrugged, but didn't turn around.

"Everything okay?"

Finally, Quinn turned, gave a noncommittal shrug, and headed toward her usual chair in the corner without a word. No sarcastic remark. No little smile. Just a tired exhale as she flopped down and tucked her legs under her.

It was a sharp contrast to the bright and fun-loving girl from yesterday.

I walked over and crouched beside her, resting my hand on the arm of the chair. "You usually have a lot of opinions around this time of day. So this quiet version of you...it's a little unsettling." I tried to keep my voice light. "Did something happen at school? What's going on?"

She let out a half-laugh, but it didn't touch the sadness in her eyes. Whatever it was that was on her mind, I could tell it was heavy. "It's nothing."

"Quinn."

She glanced at me, then at the hem of her hoodie she was worrying with her fingers. "It's just...my mom was going to come for career day next week. She promised and everything."

My chest squeezed. Quinn rarely mentioned her mother. "And now she's not?" But I didn't need to know the details to know that mother-daughter dynamics could be hard and lead to heartache. Especially for a twelve-year-old girl.

"She texted this afternoon, during last period." She didn't look up. "Something came up. Again." Her voice cracked a little on the last word, and she blinked hard.

I sank onto the ottoman beside her. "I'm sorry, Quinn. That sucks."

"It does suck."

"It really sucks."

Finally, she looked up and offered me a small smile before it disappeared again. "She always tells me she wants to come, but it's like…I don't know, something more important always comes up. A meeting. A trip. Whatever. It's always more important than me."

My heart cracked for this girl who deserved to be the most important thing in her mother's life.

"I shouldn't be surprised," Quinn continued. "I just thought…maybe this time…"

"You were excited," I said gently.

She nodded. "And now I don't have anyone to come."

"What about your dad?" Ethan did seem like the obvious choice.

"He makes beer," she said simply. "That's not really a school thing. And my uncles, well…everyone in town already knows that Uncle Brody runs the Peak to Path and Uncle Gray manages the hardware store—that's so boring. And Uncle Reid…well, he's way too big of a grump to agree to come."

I didn't bother hiding my smile. She was right. "And your Uncle Preston?"

"Does he even *have* a job?"

It was my turn to shrug.

"I'm going to be the only one there without anyone."

I watched her shrink further into herself. "You know," I said after a moment. "Bookstores are kind of a school thing. If you don't think it's too boring."

Her head shot up. "What?"

"I mean…running a bookstore is a career. I order stock, manage inventory, handle customers and all that stuff. I don't know what your mom does, but if you don't think it's too lame, I could—"

"You'd come?" She sat up straight and pulled her shoulders back. "To career day? Really?"

"If you want me to," I said. "You're kind of my favorite regular."

That got a real smile out of her.

"Thanks," she said after a moment. "That would be really cool."

"I'm glad you think that inventory management and fictional worlds are cool."

That got a laugh. A real one. "The coolest."

Her whole face softened with relief and for a moment, it was just the two of us. Me and this whip-smart, fiercely independent girl I was starting to care about more than I should.

"I'll be there," I told her. "Just tell me when and where."

I gave her shoulder a gentle squeeze before standing up. Before I could move behind the counter, she stopped me again.

"Hey, Delaney."

I lifted my eyebrow in question. She rarely used my real name.

"Can you not tell my dad about this?"

I didn't like the idea of keeping secrets from her father, but there was something in her eyes. "Why don't you want him to know?"

"It's just… I don't want it to be a big thing with him and my mom." She blew out a breath. "And, I don't think having him come to talk about beer to a bunch of sixth graders is really the best idea."

"No, probably not." I chuckled. "But you don't think he'd understand?"

Quinn shrugged. "I just don't want him to feel like he has to fix everything all the time. I mean, I'm not a kid anymore. Besides, he has enough to worry about. He doesn't need to be making a big deal about nothing, you know?"

I nodded. "I do."

She pulled the sleeves of her hoodie down over her hands and mumbled, "Don't tell him, okay?"

"I won't," I said. "Promise."

She looked up at me then, her eyes shining, but a smile on her face. "Thank you."

I winked and turned to head back toward the counter as a new customer entered the store, but the weight of the moment stayed with me.

Because saying yes to Quinn had been easy.

But walking the line between helping her out and getting too close? That was starting to feel a little bit harder every day.

Ethan

The warm, earthy smell of brewing hops filled the space. I'd moved my smaller batch brews out of the shed and into the brewery, and the new brews I'd mixed up in the tanks were ready to bottle and put into kegs.

Peaks & Brews was finally ready.

Or, almost ready.

I stood behind the bar, running my hand across the smooth, polished wood Reid had custom-made just for the space. The bar top was rustic, yet beautiful and absolutely perfect. I trailed my fingers along the newly installed tap handles, just to feel their smooth finishes one more time.

The glass on the front windows had been cleaned up, and although it was too cold now to open the doors, they would be a perfect way to bring the outside in as soon as spring rolled around again.

The signage was in place out front, and Reid had delivered the last of the tabletops yesterday. All that was left were a few final touches and one final pass with the mop before the grand opening this weekend.

"You actually did it, brother." Brody stepped through the door with another box of pint glasses in his arms. He looked around with the quiet approval that only a big brother could hand out. "I'm impressed."

"You doubted me?"

Brody laughed and slid the box onto the counter. "Nah. I knew the first time I tasted one of your shitty beers that you'd nail it."

"Thanks." I rolled my eyes. "I think."

"You have to admit, some of your first attempts weren't that great."

He wasn't wrong.

"Good thing I kept at it then?"

"Exactly," Brody said. "Because that's what you do. You're not a quitter, little brother. You've more than proved that. And now…" He moved in a slow circle, with his arms out to encompass the space. "You've done it."

"Almost." I turned my attention to wipe down the bar. Again. "I'll breathe easier once there's a line out the door."

"There will be." Brody leaned against one of the barstools. "I know you're planning to do kind of an inside/outside thing with the front garage door, but have you ever thought about an actual patio space out front?"

I looked up.

"It has potential." He shrugged. "And really, a few tables out front would draw people in. Add a few lights, some plants…could be good."

I paused, turning the idea over in my head. "Maybe." I hadn't thought about a patio space at all yet. It was enough to get the brewery up and going as it was. "Might give people a reason to hang out a little longer when the weather's nice."

"Exactly."

"I'll think about it." Might as well put *getting a patio license* on my list of things to do. I nodded, mentally adding it to the already way too long list in my brain.

Brody grabbed a bottle of water from the fridge behind the bar and twisted the cap off. "You have a big guest list for the big grand opening on Saturday?"

I blew out a breath. "Only everyone."

"That list include Delaney?"

He said it casually, but I didn't miss the way my brother wiggled his eyebrows.

"She said she'd try to swing by." I shot him a look. "Why do you ask, Brody?"

He laughed, his grin slow and knowing. "Oh, only because you've mentioned her about ten times in the last few days."

"I have not."

"You have." He stood up straight. "Just today, you talked about how much she liked the wheel you made at the fall festival." He held out a finger.

"She did."

"And then once about how Quinn was enjoying the books she'd picked out for her." He held out another finger.

"She is."

Brody grinned and added a third finger. "And then a few minutes ago, when you told me she helped you with the flyer designs."

"Well, she did." I rubbed the back of my neck and looked away. "I've been working with her. It makes sense that she'd come up."

"Or that you can't stop thinking about her."

I spun around so I could glare at him. "You done?"

"Not yet." His grin grew wider, and he laughed. "Look, man. I'm not trying to give you a hard time."

"Could have fooled me."

"I'm just saying…you like her."

I couldn't deny it. He was right. I *did* like Delaney. Hell, I couldn't stop thinking about her. Finally, I sighed, leaned on the bar and stared at the freshly polished taps. "Maybe I do."

Brody didn't say anything for a moment. "And?"

"It's not that simple."

"Sure it is. You like her. Ask her out."

It was my turn to laugh. "Says you, the man who never seems to go after the woman he's so obviously interested in." No one really understood what was going on with Brody and Lauren, but it didn't take a relationship expert to see that they were into each other.

"We're not talking about me."

"Convenient," I muttered under my breath. "Look," I said after a moment. "I can't just ask her out. We've only barely stopped bickering every time we talk. The bookstore is right next door, and that's not changing. I can't afford for us to be enemies."

"So don't screw it up."

"Right," I said, more frustrated with myself than him. "But if I do, I don't just lose a potential date. I lose a neighbor and a friend. And…"

Brody was quiet for a beat. "And Quinn?"

I nodded. "Yeah. There's that. She likes Delaney. A lot. They have this…thing. If I tried something and it didn't end well…I couldn't do that to Quinn."

Brody took a drink of his water, then set the bottle down and looked at me. "You're a great dad, Ethan. Everyone knows that. But being a good dad doesn't mean that you don't get to do things for yourself, too."

I didn't say anything.

"I'm not telling you to be reckless," he continued. "But if there is something between the two of you, don't run from it just because it's complicated."

He wasn't wrong. Still.

"She'll be at the opening?" Brody asked again.

"Yeah." I knew she wouldn't miss it.

"Maybe it's time to take the chance, brother," Brody said, his voice low. "Quinn's tougher than you think. After all, she survived you and her mother not working out."

Dammit. He had a point.

"You've built something real here, Ethan," Brody continued, slapping me on the shoulder. "You're giving that girl the stability and the future she deserves. You should be proud of that. And maybe it's time for you to stop assuming that everything good has to come with a risk attached."

I didn't respond, but simply let my brother's words settle in.

Long after Brody took his exit, his words were still swirling around in my head. For the first time all day, my to-do list was forgotten.

All I could think of was Delaney.

And what it would be like on opening day to look up and see her watching me from across the room with that gorgeous smile on her face.

What would it be like to have that smile aimed at me?

Not as a neighbor. Not as a friend.

But something more.

Chapter Nine

Delaney

The grand opening of Peaks & Brews was in full swing by the time I closed up the shop and made my way next door. The turnout to help Ethan celebrate was amazing, and it almost made me laugh to think about how against it, and him, I'd been only six weeks ago.

I still had a few concerns about how his business would affect my customers and potential customers, but now that I'd gotten to know him better and seen what a genuinely good man he was, most of the concerns had been put to bed and the smile on my face was real when I pulled open the front door and stepped inside.

The brewery was packed with people. So many bodies in a small space not only created heat, but noise, too.

As a self-declared introvert, I didn't usually go in for such big crowds, but when Ethan asked me personally if I'd be at his opening, there was no way I could say no.

People were everywhere, standing shoulder to shoulder, laughing and toasting to the new brewery with the samples in hand. There was music playing at just the right volume to provide a nice background without overwhelming the conversation.

I had to admit, Ethan had done an excellent job pulling it all together.

I stood for a moment and took in the scene before me.

Sure, it was only opening night. But by all accounts, Peaks & Brews looked like it was going to be a huge success.

"Okay, it's official." Kat appeared at my side, her baby boy in her arms. "Ethan did a great job. This place looks great. Who knew the old Chinese food place could look so good?"

I laughed and gave my new friend a side hug in greeting.

"I'm still going to miss the ginger beef, though."

"I thought this place had been closed for years."

"Still." She stared at me in faux shock. "Now I'll never have it again."

I shook my head. "You'll be glad to know then that Ethan created a ginger beer in honor of the building's roots."

Kat spun and her mouth dropped open. "He did not!"

"He did."

Kat threw her head back, her beautiful red hair cascading down her shoulders, and laughed. "Wait until I tell Andy." She blew me a kiss. "I'll see you in a bit." And then she was gone.

I watched my friend with a smile on my face. Kat was a force of nature. I had to admit, she'd been a good influence in bringing me out of my shell a little bit.

"Hey there." Lauren joined me and passed me a small tasting cup. "And IPA, I'm told," she said as I took a sip. "You okay?"

"I'm fine." I shook my head a little. "Just…there are a lot of people here."

"Right?" Together, we moved to the side and leaned up against the wall. "I feel like half the town is here. It's great."

"It is." I sipped at my beer.

Lauren raised an eyebrow. "Someone's had a change of attitude."

"How could I not? Ethan's put everything he has into this place. And it shows." Before I could say more, I spotted Quinn weaving her way through the crowd toward us.

She popped up at my side, her face flushed from excitement.

"Hey," she said, beaming up at me. "You made it."

"Of course I did. I wouldn't miss it."

"Thanks again," she said, her voice dipping a little. "For career day yesterday."

"It was my pleasure," I answered honestly. I had no idea what to expect when I arrived at the middle school, but it turned out to be a really fun afternoon, with Quinn giving a small presentation about me and what I did before I answered questions. "You rocked it. I don't think I've ever been described as a *keeper of imagination and fantasy worlds* before."

"Thanks." Quinn straightened her shoulders. "I hope it wasn't too much, but I had to make it sound super cool."

"Super cool?"

She shrugged. "Middle schoolers can be brutal."

"Fair enough. I think they liked it, though."

"They totally did."

Before she could say more, one of her friends called her name and she turned.

"Go." I waved her off.

"See you later, bookstore lady." She winked at me,

already walking backward into the crowd. "Don't leave without trying the cider. It's *so* good."

As soon as she was out of earshot, Lauren tilted her head at me. "What was that all about?"

"Career day," I said, trying not to make a big deal out of it. "I guess her mom couldn't make it last minute, so I offered to help out. No biggie."

"Seems like a biggie."

I avoided making eye contact, but when Lauren didn't elaborate after a moment, I turned to see her giving me a sharp, quiet look. A look that was maybe just a little bit too perceptive.

"What?"

"Nothing." She sipped her drink. "It's just interesting, is all."

"She's a good kid." I looked down into my glass.

"Mm-hmm."

Whatever Lauren was thinking, I did not need her to say it. My feelings were already complicated enough.

Thankfully, the crowd shifted a little bit, and through the throng of people, I spotted Ethan across the room.

For the first time all night, he wasn't surrounded by well-wishers.

He stood behind the bar, his hand resting on a beer tap. He looked good. Relaxed and completely in his element.

As if he could sense me looking, he lifted his head, and his eyes met mine. His lips curled up into a genuine smile that made something low in my gut tighten.

For a moment, I forgot my friend standing next to me, the noise, and all the people. It was just him.

I lifted my hand in a slight wave that he mirrored back at me.

"You should probably go say hello," Lauren said from beside me, a trace of humor in her voice.

I nodded and, without another word, started to move toward him.

Ethan

I took a second to lean against the bar and take it all in.

That, and breathe for a second.

I'd been going nonstop all day, trying to get the last few details ironed out before the doors opened for the grand opening. And once they did, well...to say I'd been blown away by the turnout would be an understatement. It was loud, busy, and chaotic in a way that meant people were happy and excited.

They were sampling, ordering and staying.

I knew there was support for Peaks & Brews in Trickle Creek, but I hadn't expected this. It was more than I could have hoped for.

I'd been pulled in every direction by well-wishers and my newly hired staff, who had so many questions. But for this moment, it was just me.

After months of stress, plaster dust, worry, and wondering whether I was out of my damn mind to be opening a brewery while single-handedly raising a twelve-year-old girl, I'd actually done it.

I blew out a breath.

That's when I saw her.

Delaney.

Admittedly, I'd been looking for her in the crowd all night, wondering whether she'd come. Of course she would.

She stood with Lauren against the back wall, her hair

pulled up in a ponytail, one of her oversized knit sweaters on over leggings. She was wearing earrings. That was new.

Delaney had a cup in her hand, and I couldn't help but wonder which brew she'd opted to try first. If I had to guess, it would be something light. *Maybe the wheat ale.*

Her eyes met mine, and my lips automatically curled up into a smile. When she smiled back, it hit me straight in the chest.

She lifted her hand in a little wave. An action I returned, my eyes locked on hers.

Lauren said something to her, but she didn't even turn to her friend before she started to move through the crowd.

To me.

All the people faded away as I watched her make her way through the room toward me. She reached the bar, just as I stepped around the end of it.

"Looks like the town approves." She nodded toward the packed room behind her.

"Apparently, they like the beer," I said. "What about you?" I glanced at her still mostly full cup.

"IPA." She shrugged. "I'm more of a wheat ale or pilsner girl myself."

I knew it.

Without a word, I took the glass from her and quickly poured her a sample of a brew I knew she'd enjoy more.

"Thank you." She took it with a smile. "Congratulations, Ethan," she said after taking a sip. "Seriously. The place looks amazing."

"You doubted me?"

She dropped her eyes and for a moment, I was sure she was going to deny it.

"Let's just say, I wasn't your biggest fan at first."

I couldn't help it; I laughed. "You don't say."

"It's true." She tried and failed to look serious. "But with beer like this, I have no choice but to change my mind."

I watched as she took another sip of her drink before I asked, "So, it's just the beer that changed your mind then?"

Delaney looked up at me, all traces of humor gone as she assessed me. She opened her mouth to respond, but just then, someone tapped on my shoulder. One of my newly hired bar staff, flushed and flustered and very obviously upset about something.

"Sorry to interrupt, Ethan, but we've got a problem with one of the CO2 lines. There's a jam somewhere."

Of course there was.

I turned back to Delaney. "I should…just give me a minute?"

She nodded and took a step back. "Go." She smiled. "Save the beer."

I watched her for another second before ducking behind the bar and into the back room.

The situation turned out to be a fairly easy fix, but by the time we got it cleaned up and I came out again, she was gone.

I scanned the room, looking for her, but there was no sign of her.

"Mr. Lyons?"

I turned to see my latest well-wisher, only to find Quinn's teacher, Mrs. Kelly.

"Hi there. Thanks for coming."

"Are you kidding? My husband and I are always looking for new places to try for date night. Congratulations on such a great turnout. I also wanted to thank you, or maybe I should thank Delaney."

I blinked. "Thank her? For what?"

She gave me a sideways look. "For career day yesterday.

Quinn was so proud to have her there. She gave a great presentation on how exciting it was to be a bookseller and introduced Delaney. And Delaney did such a good job, too. The kids loved her."

Career day?

Delaney?

My heart stalled.

"Oh," I said, managing to recover from my shock a little. "I didn't know…Quinn didn't mention it."

Neither did Delaney.

"Oh, I just assumed you knew." Mrs. Kelly's brow furrowed. "Quinn mentioned how busy you've been lately with…" She waved her arm around and trailed off. "Well, I'm sure she meant to say something to you and it just slipped her mind."

"Right." I forced a smile on my face. "I'm sure she did."

We exchanged a few more pleasantries before Quinn's teacher slipped back into the crowd.

I stood there, stunned for a beat. Not angry. Not really.

I just felt…something.

Delaney had stepped in for Quinn. And she hadn't told me.

Neither of them had.

Part of me hated that, for so many reasons.

But the other part of me? The part that couldn't stop picturing Delaney's soft smile and the way Quinn lit up around her?

Well, that part of me wasn't sure what to feel at all.

Delaney

I didn't bother stifling my yawn as I pulled my long hair up into a messy bun and took my contact lenses out for the evening.

Social events exhausted me at the best of times, but the brewery opening with so many people packed into a small space and...well, Ethan and whatever was going on there... had absolutely drained me.

I know I wasn't imagining the connection between us.

And that was the entire problem. And the reason I felt so unsettled.

I'd spent the better part of the evening trying to convince myself that I hadn't been impressed by this new version of him. Or at least, the new-to-me version.

Like the original opinion of him I'd built up in my head —the over-the-top charming, way too smooth and cocky version—had never really existed at all.

It would be so easy to give in to whatever it was that was happening with him. But I knew better. *Didn't I?*

I was too tired to think about it.

I tugged the oversized slouchy knit sweater that should have been thrown out ages ago, but I couldn't seem to part with, over the tank top I slept in and was just about to grab my book and climb into bed when I heard the knock.

I froze, unsure I'd heard properly.

The door that led straight up the stairs to my apartment over the shop was in the back, and hardly used considering I tended to come and go through the shop, and I rarely had visitors.

I waited for a moment. Three sharp raps. Hesitant but purposeful. I hadn't been hearing things.

I glanced at the clock. It was almost midnight.

I padded across the apartment, the old wooden floor cool under my feet, and peeked out the little window that looked down to the alley below.

Ethan.

What was he doing here?

Still in his button-down from earlier, with his sleeves rolled up, he wasn't wearing a coat. His hair was slightly mussed, like he'd run his hands through it a million times. He looked good. But also tired....and restless.

I headed down the steep back stairs to unlock the door.

"Ethan. Hey." I wrapped my sweater tightly around me, aware I was wearing little more than my pajama shorts and tank top.

"You wear glasses?"

It was the last thing I expected him to say after knocking on my door at midnight. "I do." Reflexively, I pushed my thick plastic frames up the bridge of my nose. "Is everything okay?"

"Yeah," he said. "I mean no. Not really. I don't know."

"Do you want to come in?"

He looked past me at the tiny staircase that led to my place. "No." He shook his head. "I mean, thank you. But I know it's super late, and I don't want to keep you. I should have...I mean, I can come back in the morning when—"

"No." I put a hand on his arm. "It's fine. What's going on? Is it a beer emergency?" I tried for a joke, but he didn't crack a smile.

He shook his head. "It's Quinn."

Something in my chest tightened, and the smile fell from my face. "Is she okay?"

"Yes," he said quickly, seeing my concern. "It's just...I ran into her teacher tonight," he said, his voice low. "She told me that Quinn did a great job at career day. With you."

I swallowed hard. "Oh."

"You didn't tell me."

I shook my head and wrapped my arms tighter around my waist. "Quinn asked me not to."

I didn't miss the flash of hurt in his eyes before it was replaced by something else. His jaw tightened. "And you listened to her?"

"I did. She didn't want to hurt you," I said, trying not to let my voice rise. "She was upset and disappointed with her mother and didn't want to make it your problem. She didn't want it to be a whole thing."

"And you think that stepping in without saying anything...*that's* not a whole thing?"

I bristled and took a small step back. "I was trying to help, Ethan. It's not a big deal."

"But it is," he said sharply, before catching himself. "It *is* a big deal," he tried again, his voice softer now. "Quinn tells me everything. We're a partnership."

Something inside me softened. I reached for his arm again. "You still are," I told him. "She knows how busy you've been. I really think she just didn't want to add to your worry. It was fine."

Ethan inhaled. A moment later, when he blew out his breath, there was the trace of a smile on his lips. "I know." He ran a hand through his hair. "I mean, I really do know."

I removed my hand, tightening the sweater that had slipped open.

"I'm not even mad," he said. "I just——" He stopped. "I don't know what I'm feeling."

That made two of us. Not that I was ready to volunteer that piece of information.

We stood there, the silence between us growing into something more.

"You're a great dad, Ethan," I said after a moment. "Quinn is an awesome kid. That's because of you."

He looked at me, really looked at me. My heart thudded in my chest.

"Delaney."

I swallowed hard.

He stepped closer. Just enough for the air to shift between us.

His gaze dropped to my mouth for just the briefest moment before snapping back to my eyes. "This isn't why I came here."

"Why did you come?"

"I don't know," he said, his voice low and raw. "To say thank you. To be annoyed. To ask you why you wouldn't tell me about it." He ran a hand over his face and tried again. "I came to see you."

My heart raced. It was hard to breathe.

I don't remember who moved first. Maybe we both did.

But the second his mouth was on mine, every single thing dropped away.

He kissed me like he'd been holding himself back for weeks. One hand settled on my hip, the other skimming the curve of my jaw before cupping my cheek. His touch was careful and desperate, as if he wasn't sure how long it would last.

And I kissed him back, like nothing else mattered. Not the tentative truce we'd declared. Not the new friendship we'd been building. Not the fact that neither of us could afford messy or complicated.

By the time we pulled apart, I was breathless and more than a little stunned at what had just happened.

Then he stepped back. He lifted one hand, touched his index finger to his lower lip and smiled softly. "Yeah," he murmured. "I didn't come here to do that either."

And then, before I could find my voice, he gave me one

last look, turned and disappeared into the night, leaving me staring after him.

Chapter Ten

Ethan

The wind had picked up by mid-afternoon, and with it came that sharp bite in the air that meant snow wasn't far behind. And not just a few flurries, but real snow. The kind that meant winter was really and truly here.

We were only barely into November, but Mother Nature didn't seem to care about trivial details like the date on the calendar. Life in a mountain town was unpredictable, especially when it came to the weather.

Not that I minded too much. I'd grown up spending all my free time on the ski hill, and I couldn't wait to get Quinn out there, too. On our few visits to my brothers, she'd tried it and liked it. But it was different when you lived right down the street from the ski hill.

With any luck, we'd be spending most weekends on the hill. Maybe it could be a new way for us to reconnect. Quinn had been pulling away lately, and I couldn't help but let it worry me. No matter what my brothers told me about how it was *normal* for a twelve-year-old girl to want to spend

more time with her friends than her dad. It still felt...
strange. Like the end of something.

Still, I was glad she was starting to make good friends in
Trickle Creek. I'd been so worried about the move, but she
was doing great. Coming back to town had been a good
decision for so many reasons.

I pulled my gaze from the building storm outside and
went back to wiping down the bar, not that I expected any
customers. It was the midweek lull in shoulder season. Most
of the locals had already hunkered down for what was
supposed to be the first big storm of the season, and there
weren't many tourists to speak of at this time of year, with
the golf course closed and the ski hill not quite ready to open.

Quinn had left a few hours ago with Reid for their
weekly ice cream date, opting instead for hot chocolate in
the cozy lounge of the Tamarack Inn. Too cold for cones,
they'd declared.

I left the cloth on the bar and moved to the front
window to watch the snow swirling around the deserted
plaza. There wasn't a soul out there. Which meant there was
no point staying open any longer.

I flipped the sign over the door to "Closed" and glanced
toward Plot Twist. *Was Delaney still open? Was she prepared for
the storm?*

It had been almost three weeks since I'd shown up at her
door in the middle of the night like an idiot and changed
everything between us with one kiss.

But what a kiss it was.

I'd walked away feeling as though the earth had
completely tilted under my feet.

And in the weeks since...we hadn't talked about it.

Not once.

It's not that we'd actively avoided each other either. That would be impossible in a town like Trickle Creek, especially considering we were neighbors. She'd popped into the brewery a few times. Always with friends or to say hi to Quinn. And I'd gone next door once or twice looking for my daughter, or some advice on the font for the new menu or for some other reason I'd pulled together as an excuse just to see her.

Now, when she looked at me, there was something new behind it.

A little bit guarded. But not completely.

The flirting had turned into something else, too. For one thing, there was no longer any denying that there *was* a flirtation between us.

The lingering glances that held a beat too long. The fingers that brushed my arm when I handed her a beer. The quiet smiles.

Oh yes, that was all very much there.

But still, we hadn't talked about the kiss.

What was there to say?

We were both busy. Now that Peaks & Brews was officially open for business, I had even less free time. And Quinn was and always would be my priority. Christmas was right around the corner, too. Obviously, it was a busy time for Delaney. Never mind her usual book clubs and writing groups.

Timing, as always, was a bastard.

Still, I replayed that kiss over and over in my head. And the tiny little shorts and tank top she'd been wearing. Her hair piled on top of her head, and those sexy librarian glasses over her big, green eyes.

Damn.

I'd gone to bed with that image in my head more than once.

A ping pulled me from my thoughts before they could get carried away. I pulled my phone from my back pocket.

QUINN:

> Looks like a blizzard. Uncle Reid says I can stay here tonight. I brought my book and they're all set up for a power outage.

I stared at the message for a beat. The snow had started to come down even harder since I'd been lost in my thoughts.

I sent her a quick text back.

> Sounds like a good idea. Help out if you can. Love you.

I grinned when, a second later, her reply came through.

> Of course I will! Love you, too.

A moment later, my phone buzzed again. This time with a call.

Preston.

"Hey," I answered. "What's up?"

"You're not going home tonight," he said without preamble.

"Excuse me?"

"Figured you'd want a heads-up," he said. "I just got called in for duty." Preston worked with the local search and rescue crew. When he wasn't out playing in the mountains, he was usually helping those who were. "It's going to be a busy night," he continued. "Trees are down on the main highway northbound, and Evergreen Way is a skating rink. Cars in the ditch everywhere."

I sighed. "That's the way I take home."

"Which is why I say, you're not going home tonight." There was a trace of a smile in his voice, despite the serious job he was on. "Stay put. It's a shit show out here. And the power lines are already sagging like crazy. I wouldn't be surprised to see the power go out soon."

"Shit."

"That's an understatement," he said. "The first storm of the season is always a bitch. But this one is going to be a doozy."

"Awesome," I muttered, already heading for the brew room. "I better make sure the generators are in place and double-check the tank lines."

"Good plan, brother," Preston said. "Don't risk the beer."

"Priorities."

"You know it." He laughed, but there was an edge of seriousness to his voice when he asked, "You staying there, then?"

"Looks like it." I didn't have much of a choice. "Quinn's with Reid and Avery at the inn. I'll make sure things are good here."

"Good. I'll check in later."

Before I could reply, the line went dead. Preston was in for a busy night. Not that he'd mind. He loved working with the search and rescue team. The adrenaline fueled him.

I tucked my phone in my back pocket and, with a sigh, went to check on the beer.

I had the generators in place. If the power went out, the beer would hold.

Still, I planned to keep a close eye on things. Just in case.

I leaned against the edge of a stainless-steel tank, staring at the blinking green lights and listening to the wind howl outside.

There was no going home tonight.

Delaney

There hadn't been a customer in well over two hours, and judging by the way the snow was blowing sideways through the plaza, there wasn't likely to be any.

I'd just finished locking up and was halfway through the shop to head up to my apartment when a flash of movement caught my eye.

Ethan.

He was bracing himself against the wind, snow clinging to his jacket and hood as he plowed his way through the snowdrift to the front of the shop. He tried the door and, finding it locked, rapped on the glass.

"What the—"

I moved quickly, so he didn't freeze to death, and unlocked the door. A blast of cold air rushed in with him.

"What are you doing, Ethan? You look like a snowman."

"And I only walked a few feet from my door to yours." He laughed and shook his head. "It's crazy out there."

"Which is why I ask, what are you doing?"

He brushed snow from the front of his coat and looked up. "I'm checking on you."

I took a step back, surprised. "You are?"

He chuckled. "I figured you'd already be closed up, but I saw the light and I just wanted to make sure you had everything you needed for the storm. It sounds like it's going to be a big one."

"Oh." I was touched by his thoughtfulness. "The forecast just said *snow.*" I held my fingers up in air quotes.

Ethan laughed. "The weather in the mountains is so unpredictable that the forecasters often just default to their best guess. But I just got off the phone with Preston. He works with the search and rescue crew," he added, when I looked confused. "He told me the roads are already sheer ice, people are sliding all over, there are lots of cars in the ditch already, and the snow shows no signs of stopping. Our first storm of the season will be a good one."

"Wow." I looked past him into the plaza. What was left of the afternoon sun was all but blocked by the dark clouds and the heavy snow. "I must have gotten lucky last year. We had some big snow dumps, but nothing like this." Truthfully, after my first winter in Trickle Creek, I'd been surprised there hadn't been more severe weather. "I guess I'm past due."

Ethan smiled for a moment, but his expression quickly morphed to concern. "Are you okay here? You have everything you need?"

"I do." I nodded. "What about you? Is Quinn—"

"She's with Reid and Avery at the inn. It'll be safe and warm there."

"And you?" I didn't know exactly where Ethan lived, but I did know he lived just on the edge of town. *And if the roads were already icy…* "You're not driving in this, are you?"

"Oh no." He shook his head. "I'm a confident winter driver and I have snow tires, but it's the other drivers you need to worry about." He chuckled a little. "Besides, I don't feel like adding to my little brother's workload tonight." He shrugged. "I'll stay in the brewery."

"No." My response was immediate. "You can't stay in the brewery. You'll stay here."

"Delaney. I don't want to impose on——"

"Ethan." I reached for his arm and tugged him forward. "Don't be ridiculous. There is no way I'm letting you sleep with your beer tonight. You're stuck with me."

His smile was warm and sent a thrill through me. "There are worse places to be snowed in."

I tried not to smile. "Come on upstairs," I said. "Before you track snow through my entire shop."

Chapter Eleven

Ethan

I'd never been in Delaney's little apartment before, but it was exactly how I would have pictured it. It was small. Like, really small. But it was cozy. The windows overlooking the plaza let in lots of light. Or they would have if there hadn't been a huge snowstorm raging outside.

She had a plant on the windowsill and books stacked on every available surface. Not that there were many. There was no kitchen table, just a little eating bar attached to the tiny cooking space that blended into the living room, which was only big enough for a small couch and a coffee table.

"Your place is cute." I shrugged out of my jacket and hung it on the hook in the small hallway. I'd left my boots at the bottom of the stairs by the back door, where they could dry.

"It's not much." She looked bashful but also proud. "But I don't need a lot and since I spend most of my time in the shop anyway…"

"I really like it."

"Thank you," she said softly. She held my gaze for a moment before quickly looking away. "I was just going to heat up some stew I had in the freezer." She turned away and busied herself in the small kitchen. "It seemed like a perfect snowy night meal. I have enough for two, if you're hungry."

"That sounds perfect." I stepped out of her way. "We should probably eat before the power goes out."

"The power?" She looked over her shoulder, worry on her face. "You think it'll go out?"

"There's a good chance for sure." I glanced out the window. "Preston said the lines are already heavy with ice, so I wouldn't be surprised."

"Well, this won't take long. Make yourself at home."

Delaney was already moving around the little kitchen, pulling together the makings of a meal. I couldn't stop watching her.

She wore another of her oversized sweater jacket things over a black shirt and jeans. Since coming upstairs, she'd pulled her long hair up into a messy bun and pushed her sleeves up. She looked relaxed and at ease in her natural habitat.

And softer than the sharp, confident woman who single-handedly ran Plot Twist.

It was yet another version of her. Another version that I couldn't tear my eyes away from.

"I have some candles in the hutch over there," she said, grabbing my attention. "Just in case the power goes out."

"It's not a bad idea." I followed her directions and found a selection of candles just where she instructed. Some tea lights in mismatched holders, a few tapers, and one vanilla-scented one in a jar that looked like it had been a gift.

I set them all on the coffee table as she joined me with

two bowls of stew. "Sorry," she said. "I don't have a table, so this will have to do." She tossed two oversized pillows on the floor to act as chairs right as the lights overhead flickered once, twice, and then stayed out.

"Well, that didn't take long."

She laughed. "Good thing we're ready."

Together, we lit the collection of candles and settled onto the floor to eat in the warm glow of candlelight.

The stew was delicious. Thick and meaty and home-made. It was easily the best thing I'd eaten in weeks. "Did you make this?"

She shrugged. "I like to cook, but it's usually only me, so I freeze a lot of leftovers."

"It's delicious." I took another big bite. "If you ever want someone to share with…" I trailed off, unsure of how to finish the thought.

"I'll keep that in mind." Delaney smiled as she put a spoonful in her mouth.

"We should have a drink," I said, only half joking.

She gave me a look. "Please don't suggest beer. No offense."

"None taken." I laughed. "And no, I could use a break from beer myself."

"What about wine?" She got to her feet. "I think I have a bottle of red."

"Perfect."

A moment later, she handed me a glass and settled back onto her pillow, cross-legged.

"To snowstorms." I held out my glass.

She hesitated for a moment before clinking her glass to mine. "To snowstorms."

We settled into our meals, sipping our wine as we finished dinner and talked.

First, about the storm and what kind of winter we each thought we'd have. She asked about the brewery, and I asked about book sales.

And then she mentioned Ontario.

"You're from there?"

Delaney nodded. "I ran a little shop out there. Nook & Nest."

"Sounds cute."

"It was." She pushed her empty bowl to the middle of the table and leaned back on her arms. "It was mostly home decor and some local art and things. I loved it."

"What happened? How did you end up out West?"

She was quiet, and for a moment, I wasn't sure she was going to answer me. Then she sighed. "My ex-husband. He made a lot of bad decisions, promised a lot of things to a lot of people. Promises he couldn't keep. Especially not to me." She lifted her wine to her mouth. "I lost everything."

"Delaney. I'm sorry."

She took a sip and put her glass down before looking at me with a small smile. "So was I," she said. "At first. But I worked hard to build my credit up again and put together some savings. Now I live here, and I have Plot Twist. I wouldn't change anything."

Maybe I shouldn't have asked, but I needed to know. "And your husband?"

"*Ex*," she said pointedly. "I haven't spoken to him in years. Last I heard, he was out East still. And if I know Ken at all, he's still trying to charm his way through life."

Charm.

All of a sudden, it made sense why, when we'd first met, Delaney continually called me out for being too charming and why she never fell for my smooth moves. I almost laughed, and she must have realized that I'd put two and two together, because before I could ask, she said, "No, I don't think you're anything like him. Not now," she added.

"But at first?"

Delaney shrugged. "Can you blame me? A good-looking, way too smooth, charming man trying to get me to do what he wanted…"

"Good-looking?"

She rolled her eyes, and I grinned. "No," I said. "I guess I can't blame you at all. But in my defense, I didn't know about your ex."

"Would it have made a difference?" She tilted her head and gave me a wry smile. "Tell me about Quinn's mom."

I probably shouldn't have been surprised by the question. After all, Delaney did spend a lot of time with Quinn, and there was the whole career day letdown.

"Unless you don't want to talk about it," she said quickly. "I understand if—"

"It's not that." I stopped her. The last thing I wanted was for Delaney to think there was anything left between Polly and me. There most certainly wasn't and hadn't been for longer than I cared to think about. "I was just a little surprised by the question, is all."

"You were? Really?" A smile teased at her lips.

"Only because…well, I don't give her much thought, if I'm being honest. Not beyond the fact that she's Quinn's mom." I shrugged. "She's kind of self-selected her way out of our lives."

"That's so sad," Delaney said. "For Quinn."

I couldn't help but grin a little. "For Quinn," I agreed. "Definitely. But sadly, she's mostly used to her mother's absence by now. It's been this way almost from the beginning."

"Even when she was a baby?" We'd long since pushed

the coffee table out of the way and brought a battery-powered space heater upstairs to keep us warm. Delaney turned so she was facing me, cross-legged. "Surely, when Quinn was…"

She trailed off when I shook my head.

Delaney

My heart ached for a little girl who had an absent mother. And for Ethan, too. It couldn't have been easy to raise a daughter with a partner who was uninvested.

"It's okay," he said with a small smile. "Polly and I should never have been married. We were never right for each other, only by the time we realized it, we'd been married a little over a year, and Polly was pregnant. We tried to make it work. For Quinn's sake." He chuckled a little. "We tried *way* too long, and it was never going to work. Truth be told, we should have called it years earlier than we did, but…"

"But you didn't want to give up." I reached for him and took his hand as if it were the most natural thing in the world.

He glanced at our hands and then back at me. "Exactly," he said after a moment. "You never get married thinking it will end in divorce. Especially when you have a kid to think about. But ultimately, we decided it was probably best to model single parenting instead of…well, whatever it was that we were doing." He chuckled softly, the sound low and self-deprecating. "It's funny, because it's not like things didn't work out because one of us cheated or anything. In many ways, that might have been easier. It might have made more sense."

I stayed silent, giving him the space he needed. I got the

sense that he didn't speak about the situation very often. If at all.

"We weren't angry all the time," he added after a beat. "We only really fought when she let Quinn down, which she started to do more and more. Her career is the most important thing in Polly's life. I guess I thought it might change after Quinn was born, but it was almost like it became even more important. I was building a career, too. But when Quinn came along, the world of finance didn't hold the same appeal, so I opted to stay home with her.

"Polly was just so driven, but in a way that wasn't healthy. For a while, I wondered whether she'd applied that same drive to our marriage if it might have worked, but I don't think it would have. We are fundamentally very different people. By the end, there wasn't any love between us. It was just…cold."

He drifted off, his gaze moving past me as if he were seeing something that was no longer there. After a moment, he shook his head and looked at me again with a small smile. "And that's no way for a little girl to grow up, so…" He held up his free hand and dropped it with a shrug. "Here we are."

"Here you are." I offered him a smile and added, "She's lucky to have you."

"I'm lucky to have her."

The candlelight flickered between us, and I realized I was holding my breath.

Maybe it was the storm. Or the wine.

Maybe it was the way we were finally opening up and getting to know each other properly.

But right at that moment, cross-legged on my living room floor with the storm raging just outside the window and the world shrinking between us, I wanted to tell him everything.

Things I'd never told anyone before.

The way I knew how it felt to be someone's afterthought.

How I'd also spent way too long in a marriage that I knew wasn't right. And I'd spent far too long convincing myself I didn't need anyone in my life. That I would be perfectly fine on my own.

How terrifying it was to realize that maybe I *did* want more.

And maybe the man I wanted it with sat right in front of me.

I didn't say any of that.

Instead, I readjusted my hand in his and squeezed a little.

He squeezed back.

"Do you ever regret it?" I asked, my voice barely above a whisper.

"Which part?"

My lips curled up in a small smile. "Any of it?"

"No." His answer was immediate. "It's true we should never have been married," he continued. "But if I hadn't married Polly, I wouldn't have Quinn, and she's the best thing that's ever happened to me."

The way he said it with such solid certainty felt right.

"You?"

I'd been expecting the question, but it still stopped me. After a second, I shook my head. "I used to," I answered honestly. "There was a time when I was so mad at myself for falling for Ken's charm and losing everything to a man who never could have loved me the way I loved him."

"And now?"

"And now, I know that if things hadn't happened just the way they did, I wouldn't be right here, right now."

Ethan's smile made my stomach flip, and when he scooted closer to me until our knees touched, my breath caught in my throat.

His eyes darkened in the soft light and for a second, I thought he might say something else. Instead, he leaned in.

When his mouth found mine, there was no hesitation.

Only heat.

And the desperate, terrifying, beautiful feeling of falling.

Chapter Twelve

Ethan

The old windows rattled from the icy winds outside. The snow was piling up, blurring the world beyond Delaney's tiny apartment.

But all I could see was her.

Delaney was the only thing that mattered.

Soft and real and returning my kiss as if she'd been waiting just as long as I had for this moment.

This wasn't a stolen kiss in the back alley in the middle of the night. This was real. This was just us finally giving in to what had been building from the first time she'd burst into my construction site, all fired up about the noise.

My hands slid over her, slow and careful, testing. Her oversized sweater that I was going to be more than happy to rid her of slipped from her shoulder, revealing the fitted T-shirt underneath. With a little tug, I relieved her of the sweater and skimmed my hands up and over the soft fabric of the shirt that hugged all her curves.

Her hands weren't tentative either. They gripped my

shirt, sliding beneath the hem. Her touch was confident as they spread over my abs.

I groaned at her touch. God help me, it had been so long since I'd let anyone get close like this.

Since I even wanted to.

I sat back a little, tugging my shirt off and over my head, tossing it somewhere behind me. The heat between us was all I needed.

And I needed a lot more of it.

The candlelight danced across her features. Her hair was piled up in a messy bun, her lips slightly parted, and her breath coming quickly.

"You're beautiful," I said, my voice rough and only barely controlled. "You have no idea."

"You're not so bad yourself." She pulled me back to her, kissing me deeper than before, a moan slipping from her mouth that had my cock rock hard in my jeans.

She pulled away with a gasp. "I...this..." She rocked back on her heels and bit her bottom lip. "I just...this is all so..."

"Do you want me to stop?"

"No." Her answer was immediate. "Not even a little." Her sly smile told me she meant it. "I'm just...it's been a while, is all."

Her admission made me want her even more.

"For me, too."

She lifted her eyebrow in question. "But you're so—"

"Charming?" I winked, and she laughed with a nod. "Yes."

"I can't argue with that," I told her. "But that's not my style. Besides, I've been pretty busy with...well, life lately."

Her eyes flashed, and without another word, her hands went to the hem of her shirt. She pulled it over her head.

I sucked in a breath. She was stunning. I couldn't keep my hands off her a moment longer.

Once more, I closed the distance between us, pressing my bare skin against hers, the lace of her pale-pink bra scratching my skin. I kissed her until she was breathless before I dipped my lips to the base of her neck.

She shivered under my touch as I reached around to unclasp her bra and slid it from her arms.

Delaney tugged at my belt, her fingers fumbling with the fly of my jeans until I took over. I stood long enough to shed my jeans, leaving my boxer briefs on, and I rejoined her on our nest of blankets on the floor.

Her breath hitched in her chest when I pressed closer and guided her down to the blankets.

She blinked up at me, her chest rising and falling fast, her lips parted in need that matched my own, her hair spilling out around her face. She looked wild, free, and so undeniably sexy I could hardly breathe.

I kissed her again—deeper this time, letting her feel everything I hadn't dared say out loud yet.

Unable to hold back, I let my lips travel down her body. To her collarbone, and then each of her luscious breasts. I kissed and sucked until she writhed beneath me.

"Ethan," she groaned my name.

"You want me to stop?"

"Are you serious right now?"

I grinned up at her and resumed my kisses that were driving us both crazy.

Her hands skimmed down my body to the waistband of my boxer briefs. She hesitated a second before they slipped beneath the elastic and cupped my ass.

It was my turn to groan. "You're killing me, woman."

"Good."

"And you are still wearing far too many clothes."

Her mischievous smile danced on her face as I unbuttoned her jeans and pulled them down, along with her matching pale-pink panties, with one sharp tug.

"Better." I sat up and admired the beautiful woman before me. "Much better."

She reached for me, but I caught her hands in mine and dropped my body over hers, pulling her arms over her head. "Patience. We have all night."

Her nostrils flared. "Promise?"

"Most definitely." I kissed her again, rougher this time, our bodies fitting together as if they were made to. I released my grip on her because I needed both hands to explore every inch of her gorgeous body.

The world outside could have vanished under all the snow, but I wouldn't have noticed. The only thing I could focus on was the sweet sounds coming from Delaney as I searched for and discovered one sensitive spot after another.

I moved lower, working my way down her body, kissing across her stomach and my hands smoothing over her hips. She shivered beneath me, but not from the cold. There was no lack of heat between us.

By the time I nudged her thighs apart and kissed my way even lower, she was trembling. "Yes," she moaned. "Oh, yes. Ethan."

Fuck, I loved the way my name sounded on her desire-soaked lips.

Her hands threaded through my hair, holding me close but not pushing me away.

I skimmed my hands up each of her bare thighs, taking in the sight of her spread out for me. Totally exposed.

It was intoxicating.

Her lips parted in a shaky breath. Her eyes were wide and clear in the candlelight. She was beyond perfection.

I trailed my fingers slowly up her inner thighs to her sweet mound, savoring the way she gasped and her fingers tightened in my hair.

She shifted, her muscles tensing beneath the kisses I trailed up her leg. I nipped gently at the soft skin, feeling her body shudder in response.

God, I was totally consumed by this woman.

When I finally pressed my mouth to her, her hips jolted and she let out a broken cry that shot straight through me.

I took my time.

Kissing, sucking, blowing, learning every reaction and every little gasp. I meant what I'd said. We had all night. And I fully intended to use it.

There was nowhere else I wanted to be except right there with her on the floor of her tiny apartment, slowly unraveling her until she came apart from my kisses.

She writhed against me, her hips lifting, chasing her need.

I gave her exactly what she craved. Slow at first, teasing and coaxing her higher and higher. And then firmer, deeper until her whole body shook and she clutched at the blankets beneath her, trying to hold back her whimpers.

"Let me hear you, baby," I told her. "Don't hold back."

Her next groan was louder, followed by a gasp when I slipped a finger into her heat. "Oh, God. Ethan...I'm going to…"

"Fuck yes, you are. Come for me, baby."

And she did.

She cried out, her body arching against my touch as her orgasm shattered her.

My cock throbbed heavy with need and a desperation to join her in her pleasure.

But not yet.

I pressed my mouth to her sweet core, savoring the taste of her as I kissed her through the rest of her orgasm. Slow and lingering, easing her down from the high and letting her know exactly how much I wanted her.

When she finally went limp beneath me, I took my time working my way back up her body with small kisses. By the time I finally reached her lips, her smile was shy, but satisfied. She pulled me into a kiss that told me without words exactly how much she'd needed this.

Needed me.

And we weren't anywhere near done.

Delaney

I wasn't sure I'd ever catch my breath again.

Nor did I want to. Because…damn. I had *not* been expecting that when Ethan stepped into my shop.

I blinked up at him as he hovered over me, bracing himself on his forearms. His hair was a very sexy mess, mussed from my fingers tugging through his locks.

His mouth was just a few inches from mine, his breath and skin warm against mine.

I slid my hands up his back, feeling the tension in his muscles. A reminder that he was still holding himself back. "Well, that was…"

"Just the beginning, baby."

His words sent a fresh rush of heat between my legs.

"If you're up for it, that is."

"Oh," I tightened my grip on his back, "I am very much up for it."

His lips curled up into a grin. He looked down on me with hunger in his eyes that I'd never seen before. "I am very happy to hear that."

Ethan's grin faded into something softer as he kissed me again, slower this time. I sank into the kiss.

He shifted, reaching between us, and my breath caught when I felt the press of his hard cock against my sensitive core.

"Still with me?"

I nodded, pulling him closer. "I'm not going anywhere."

He hesitated, a groan slipping from his lips as he looked up again. "Delaney, I'm sorry. I don't have a—"

"It's okay," I told him. "I'm on the Pill." It wasn't even something I'd thought about. Especially after our earlier confessions.

He kissed me. His mouth consumed me and caught the gasp that slipped from my lungs when he pushed into me.

I sucked in a breath, adjusting to the slow, steady stretch of him.

"Delaney." Ethan rested his forehead against mine, as if he couldn't bear to be any farther away. "You feel so good." His voice was rough, barely controlled. "So fucking perfect."

We were so in tune, he read every move of my body. Every soft sound that slipped from my lips. When I tightened my grip on his shoulders, Ethan stilled for a moment. His fingers traced lazy circles on my hip, waiting for me to move again.

I lifted my hips, pressing up to him, and the low sound he made tugged something deep in my belly.

It wasn't just physical between us. There was so much more between us, so much we hadn't said. But at least in that moment, there was nothing that needed to be said out loud.

It didn't take long for my body to tighten around him. Heat curled inside me with every slow slide, every soft brush of his lips on my neck.

When he shifted his angle slightly, I gasped as he hit a brand-new spot inside me. Reflexively, my legs wrapped around his waist.

"You like that." It wasn't a question, but I answered with a slight nod and pulled him down to my lips in a kiss that was anything but soft and careful.

When I rocked against him, urging him deeper, he cursed softly against my lips. "Delaney, I'm going to lose control."

"Good."

That was all it took for him to finally give in.

Ethan moved faster.

Harder.

Deeper.

Until I was moaning and squirming beneath him, unable to hold back the orgasm that was building up stronger inside me.

Every time he moved, it sent another wave of desire through me until I didn't think I'd be able to hold back much longer.

I knew he was close, too. He buried his head in my neck, breathing hard. He braced himself with one hand, while the other locked onto my hip as if he needed to hold on or lose himself completely.

"Delaney," he whispered, his voice strained. "Let go, baby. Come for me."

I didn't need to be told twice.

I broke apart with a cry. My body clenched tight around him, the pleasure tearing through me in sharp, blinding waves that felt like they'd never end.

He was right behind me with his own release. Ethan shuddered and moaned as he let go, his grip never wavering.

Afterward, we lay tangled together, breathing hard on our pile of blankets. The candles burned low, their glow starting to flicker. Slowly, I registered the storm outside was still battering the old glass panes. But we were warm and cozy inside.

Ethan moved to his back and pulled me over, so I lay on his chest.

He wrapped his arms tighter around me and stroked the mess of my hair off my forehead.

Neither of us spoke for a long while.

There was nothing to say.

Just when I thought he must have fallen asleep, he shifted beneath me enough that I lifted my head to look at him.

"So, I guess that kiss the other night," I started. "It meant something after all."

Ethan's smile was lazy, but satisfied. He stroked a piece of hair from my face and cupped my cheek. "I think it's safe to say it meant something, all right."

"Thought so," I teased.

"You are amazing, Delaney," he said softly. "In every single way."

I couldn't help but chuckle a little, but I meant it when I replied, "And you are very charming, Ethan. In every single way."

Only this time, when I put my head down on his chest again and let him cuddle me close, I no longer thought of that charm as a bad thing.

Not at all.

Chapter Thirteen

Ethan

When I woke, she was still in my arms, her chest rising and falling with each soft, slumbering breath. At some point in the night, we got off the floor and moved to Delaney's bed in the back of her apartment and piled the blankets high over top of us to keep us warm.

Not that we'd needed them. The heat between us was more than enough to ward off the cold. Even with the power outage keeping the heat off for most of the night.

I watched her for a few minutes, memorizing how peaceful and absolutely stunning she was.

Outside, the storm had stopped and the sun was trying to shine through the clouds. The last thing I wanted to do was look outside to see what kind of mess Mother Nature had left for us to clean up. In a perfect world, I would stay exactly where I was—in Delaney's bed, with her cuddled up on me, all day.

Sadly, that wasn't reality.

She must have sensed the shift in me, because before I

could slip away, leaving her undisturbed, Delaney's eyes fluttered open. I watched as a look of surprise crossed her features, before melting into a smile as she remembered the night before.

Her beautiful, sleepy smile stirred me to life when she looked up at me and said, "Good morning."

I pressed my lips to hers. "Good morning, beautiful. Did you sleep well?"

Her answer was a contented moan, and she wiggled closer to me.

My cock stiffened in response to the feel of her hot, bare skin on mine.

It was my turn to moan. As much as I wanted to give in to my urges—and I very much did—I'd already heard my phone binging with messages from the other room. I needed to get up and check on things. It was bad enough I'd completely forgotten to go back to the brewery and check on the tanks one last time before going to sleep. I'd been more than a little distracted. In the very best way.

But still.

I couldn't completely ignore my responsibilities.

"Looks like the storm stopped," Delaney said without lifting her head. "How bad do you think it is out there?"

"I'm not sure," I answered honestly. "But unfortunately, I'm going to need to find out sooner rather than later."

She sat up, her long, dark hair falling over her bare shoulders as she pulled the sheet up to cover her breasts. Mussed from sleep and sex, she'd never looked more beautiful than she did in that moment.

It took all my self-control not to pull the sheet down and ravage her all over again.

I swallowed hard and forced the thoughts from my head.

"You need to go check on your tanks." It wasn't a question. Delaney bit her bottom lip and nodded. "Do you think they're okay?"

"I sure hope so." Reluctantly, I flipped the cover back. Before I moved, I leaned over and gave Delaney a long, slow kiss.

"Oh. I should brush my teeth."

I chuckled. "I love the way you taste." I wiggled my eyebrows, and she blushed a very pretty shade of pink and swatted my chest as I slipped from the bed.

"You're leaving?"

"Not for long," I said, my voice low. "But I do need to make sure the tanks are okay and check in with Quinn."

Quinn.

Saying her name out loud brought the reality of my daughter sharp and pressing to the front of my mind.

What the hell were we going to tell her?

I stared at Delaney for a moment, the expression on her face matching the thoughts swirling through my head.

Nothing, I decided. We weren't going to tell Quinn anything. At least not yet. Not until I knew for sure that this thing with Delaney was more than a storm and being snowed in together.

I blinked and put a smile on my face. "I'm sure she had a great time at the inn last night with Reid and Avery, and no doubt she'll want to stay. But she tends to worry about me."

"Of course she does." The worry slipped from Delaney's face.

We'd have to talk about...well, *everything.* But it would have to wait.

"You have coffee, right?"

She smiled again, sleepy and soft. "You know I do. But I'm afraid that's probably all I have as far as breakfast goes."

"Coffee is perfect." I bent and kissed her once more, reluctant to leave her and this moment together. "I'll be back as soon as I can."

Before I caved in completely and climbed back into bed with her, I forced myself to get up, find my clothes, and face the world outside.

How WAS something that looked so light and fluffy so damn heavy?

I heaved another shovel of wet snow out of my path and, after what felt like hours, made my way to the back door of the brewery.

My gloves were soaked, and I was sweating so much I hardly needed a jacket against the sharp morning air by the time I unlocked the door.

The plows would be by to clear the back alley and most of the plaza, thank goodness, because I didn't know whether I could face the prospect of digging out the entire shop front, too.

As heavy and problematic as a heavy snowstorm was, I had to admit, it was pretty.

There was nothing quite as serene as the morning after a fresh snow, and this one was no exception.

The thick, white blanket coated every surface in white crystals that sparkled in the sunshine. It looked like a postcard.

Beautiful, yes.

But still a giant pain in my ass.

Once I finally made it inside, I stamped the snow off my boots and shed my jacket, hanging it over a stack of kegs.

The faint hum of the backup generators still filled the air around me and made me smile.

The tanks would be just fine despite my total negligence the night before.

A quick check proved me right.

Temperatures held steady, and the pressure gauges were right where they should be.

I took a few minutes to move through the brewery, checking lines, making notes and doing my usual morning duties.

I was doing everything I was supposed to do. Things I'd done hundreds of times before. But I was totally on autopilot, because the only thing I could concentrate on was the one thing, or rather, one person, I'd left next door.

Delaney.

My mind continued to travel back to the image of her curled up under the blankets: cozy, warm, and…deliciously naked.

The smile on her face when I kissed her. Like she was just as happy with the new development in our relationship as I was.

I shook my head, dragging a hand over my jaw and the stubble that over the last few weeks had started to become a full-on beard. I was really and truly settling into mountain life.

I laughed at myself and was still chuckling a moment later when my phone rang and I answered my brother's call.

"Reid." I tucked the phone between my shoulder and neck as I scribbled one final note on my clipboard. "You guys make out okay last night?"

"I was calling to ask you the same thing," my brother said. "We're good here. Had a big fire in the great room. Quinn helped us serve hot chocolate and make s'mores with the guests last night. Everyone had a good time." He paused for a moment. "Looks like there are some branches down outside, but nothing crazy. How are things there? Generators hold?"

"They did." I nodded and took another glance around the space. "It's like nothing ever happened here. If you don't count the four feet of snowdrifts outside my front door," I added as I moved out of the back room into the front of the brewery and saw the drifts outside for the first time. "Wow. The plows will have their work cut out for them."

There was no way any customers were getting through that. Not that I expected any anyway. The entire town would be digging out from the storm all day.

"Quinn good?" I asked. "I hope she wasn't too much trouble."

"Are you kidding?" My brother almost sounded angry at my question. "Quinn's great and you know it."

I chuckled. I *did* know it.

"She was a huge help last night. And I think she had fun. She's sleeping in this morning, but she was excited to help Avery make pancakes this morning."

"I'm sure she did." My kid was pretty great. And I never had to worry about her behaving herself or being a nuisance. Especially with her uncles.

"In fact, I'm keeping her today," Reid continued. "I talked to Preston earlier and he said the roads were still a total shit show. There's no point in trying to take her home to be stranded on the edge of town until the roads get better. If she stays with me, she can still make it to school if it opens tomorrow."

"I assume today is a snow day?"

"Sounds like it."

"Okay," I agreed. "If she's happy to stay and you're

good with it, she might as well hang out there. I'll give her a call later when she's up."

Reid grunted his approval. "What about you?" he asked after a moment. "Were you stuck at the brewery all night?"

I hesitated.

"I stayed at Delaney's," I admitted.

There was a beat of silence. Then a low whistle. "You did, did you?"

I could picture the smug grin on my brother's face as he no doubt painted his own picture of what exactly went on, which I was sure wasn't too far from the truth in this particular case. Not that he needed to know that.

"It wasn't like that," I said after a moment, lying straight through my teeth.

"Right." I could almost hear his eyes rolling. "I'm sure it wasn't."

"Reid." I straightened up and set the clipboard down on the bar top. "Don't say anything about it, okay? Especially not to Quinn."

"Oh?" His voice immediately sobered.

"Yeah, oh." I exhaled and pinched the bridge of my nose. "It's just all really new and I don't know...well, we don't know..."

"Of course I won't say anything," he said, and I believed him.

My brother might be the grouchiest guy in town, but he had his soft spots, and my kid was one of them.

"You like her."

"Yeah," I said, the word rougher than I meant it to be. "I do."

It was the truth. I *did* like her.

There was another pause and for a minute, I thought we

might have been disconnected. "You deserve good things, man," Reid finally said. "So does Quinn."

"She does."

"So do you," my brother said more forcefully. "You don't win any prizes putting your own life on hold any longer than you already have."

"I know."

But I didn't. Not really. From the moment I'd found out Polly was pregnant, it had always been about Quinn. Every single thing I'd ever done. Every decision. Every move. It had been for Quinn. I wasn't sure I knew how to put my own needs first.

Or whether I should.

The idea of blending my life—my *daughter's* life—with anyone else was overwhelming and more than a little bit terrifying. But I didn't need to think about that. Not yet.

Sensing I was done with the topic, Reid broke the silence that had developed over the line. "I'll check in with you later," Reid said. "Let me know if you need anything, and be safe if you go out there."

"You too, brother. Thanks."

I ended the call and leaned up against the bar, staring out the front windows at the winter wonderland outside.

I thought about Delaney's smile when I promised her I'd be back for breakfast.

About how fucking amazing it had been to have her in my arms. To kiss her. To make her cry out.

About how damn easy it had been to fall asleep with her in my arms.

And just how hard it had been to leave her side this morning.

Maybe Reid was right.

Maybe I *did* deserve good things.

Delaney was definitely a good thing.

A *very* good thing.

But it wasn't just me I needed to think about anymore. If I let someone in and it all fell apart, what about Quinn? She already loved Delaney. Probably more than she was letting on.

If I screwed this up, or if Delaney changed her mind or decided we weren't worth the trouble, what would that do to my kid?

Her mother had already let her down more times than was fair.

I wasn't sure she could handle any more disappointment.

And I wasn't so sure I could either.

Delaney

Ethan had been gone for thirty minutes already. Longer than I'd expected.

Hopefully, things were okay with his tanks. The storm had been a bad one. I didn't know enough—or anything, really—about how a long power outage would affect beer. But it probably wasn't good.

I pulled my old sweater tighter around me to ward off the chill that raced through me.

The power had come back on at some point before we'd woken. My little apartment was starting to warm up again, but that's not why I shivered.

From the moment the door had shut behind Ethan this morning, I'd been worried.

About the cold.

The effects of the storm.

Us.

That was the big one.

What happened between us had been amazing and perfect in so many ways. But also totally unplanned. And as amazing as it had been to wake up in his arms with the heat of him wrapped around me—and it had—we didn't have a chance to talk about what happened. Or what it might mean.

It did mean something, didn't it?

It had to.

At least for me. I didn't sleep with men without—*no*.

I forced myself to stop spinning out of control and focused once more on the task at hand.

Coffee.

Ethan *was* coming back. He'd told me so. I had no reason not to believe him.

I set the water on to boil and moved to the front window that overlooked the plaza.

A thick, white blanket coated absolutely everything. Huge drifts had blown up against the doors and windows of the shops. From where I stood, I couldn't even see the gazebo at the far end of the plaza.

I saw a flash of movement below.

Ethan.

He was bundled up in his parka with a shovel in hand.

He tackled the massive amount of snow in front of his shop before he moved to do mine next. He'd just started on what looked to be a never-ending task when a little snow-plow appeared around the corner, along with a few other men I couldn't recognize in their winter gear.

As if Ethan could sense me watching, he looked up and smiled.

I lifted a hand in a wave, a smile of my own taking over my face.

He was definitely going to be a bit longer still, so I turned my attention to making coffee and trying to find something besides leftover stew for us to eat when he returned.

I was curled up on the couch with a book when, almost an hour later, I finally heard a knock on my door, followed by Ethan's voice. "I'm back."

My heart skipped at the sound. "Hey." I set my book down and turned to see him still wearing his puffy jacket with a knit tuque on his head and a brown bag in his hands. "How was it out there?"

I felt a flash of guilt for not helping out, but given that I only had a very small, and totally inadequate shovel, I probably wouldn't have done much more than get in the way.

I left the couch and moved across the room.

"There is *a lot* of snow out there." He laughed as he slipped out of his coat and hung it on a hook before pulling me in for a kiss. "Mm," he murmured when he pulled away. "But that was very nice."

He reached to pull me in again, but I laughed and reached for the bag as my stomach growled. "Don't tell me this is from the Bean Bag."

"Then I won't tell you that." He winked and moved into the small kitchen where the pot of coffee was waiting for him. "But Dale managed to make it through the snow to whip up some scones for the snow removal crew, and I convinced her to sneak me a few extra."

My mouth watered as I slid the fresh pastries from the bag onto a plate.

"It was either that or we were going to be trekking through the snow to the inn where Reid and Avery are serving up pancakes, but I thought this would be better."

He gave me a heated look, and my stomach flipped.

"This is much better."

We settled on the couch—mugs of coffee in hand, the plates of scones on the coffee table—and just like that, all the worry, doubts, and stress that I'd let sneak in, even a little bit, evaporated.

Being with Ethan like that was quiet in a comfortable and easy kind of way. There was no need to speak or fill the moment with conversation. It was quiet in a way I hadn't realized I missed.

Ethan leaned back and draped one arm loosely over the back of the couch. His fingers brushed my shoulder easily. Naturally.

I put a piece of the cinnamon swirl scone in my mouth, closing my eyes to better enjoy the flaky pastry. "Oh my God, this scone is *so* good."

"*This* is so good."

My eyes popped open. I shifted in my seat to see him grinning. "It is, isn't it?" I asked.

"It really is." He nodded. "And last night was…"

"Pretty good, too."

Ethan laughed. "It was a whole lot better than good."

"Yeah. It was." I leaned my head to his shoulder and took a slow breath, breathing in the moment before returning to my coffee.

We fell into another stretch of silence that wasn't uncomfortable, but instead felt like we were both trying to figure out what might come next without saying it out loud.

Finally, Ethan cleared his throat. "About Quinn."

I tensed, just a little, my fingers tightening around my mug.

"I think maybe we shouldn't say anything to her yet," he said. "At least not until we…"

"Know what this is?"

"Exactly." He nodded. "It's just that I haven't really dated at all since her mother and...well, we're in some uncharted territory here. I just want to make sure I handle it properly, is all."

He didn't sound uncertain, just careful. I already knew that Ethan was an excellent father, but seeing the way he was so considerate and careful about Quinn's feelings made sense.

And really, I couldn't blame him for being cautious. Quinn was his daughter.

Still, it settled in my chest like something sharp.

I swallowed hard. "Sure," I said. "That makes sense."

Ethan looked at me for a second longer, as though he could tell that his request hadn't landed the way he'd expected it to. But instead of pushing the issue, he reached out and brushed a finger over the back of my hand.

A small gesture.

One that told me he *did* care.

Even if he wasn't ready to say it out loud yet.

Chapter Fourteen

Delaney

The chocolate chip, salted caramel cookies smelled so good as I pulled them from the oven, I was tempted to keep a few for myself. Ultimately, I gave in to "taste testing" one of them before putting the rest of the mostly cooled treats into a container and taking them next door.

Ethan looked up from behind the counter, a white bar towel slung over his shoulder and his hair a little messy as if he'd already run his hands through it a hundred times. The scruff of his beard that he'd been growing was getting thicker—and sexier.

I swallowed down the surge of desire that arose just from setting eyes on him.

His eyes lit up when he saw me, his own desire reflected back at me. "Hey, neighbor." He greeted me innocently, his eyes darting to his left, where I saw Quinn sitting with headphones on, doing homework.

I smiled in response and lifted the container of cookies.

"You didn't?" He moved around the counter to greet

me, wiping his hands on the towel. He stopped just before pulling me into a hug.

"I did."

"That was a joke," he said. "I was just going to make popcorn or grab some pretzels or something."

"Hey, you said you were in charge of snacks for movie night but didn't have time to do anything good. So I thought I'd help. Snack duty is a very serious thing."

I moved past him and set the cookies on the counter. Keeping distance from Ethan, when all I wanted to do was rush into his arms and press a kiss on his lips, was probably the safest move.

Quinn lifted her head from her book, her nose twitching; her eyes wide, as she pulled the headphones off her ears. "Cookies?"

I nodded.

"*Homemade* cookies?"

I nodded again, my grin taking over my face.

"I mean, I've heard about people who make cookies, but…" She lifted a corner of the lid, but Ethan pressed it down again. "Hey!"

"Those are for movie night."

"No fair."

I laughed. "You should probably try one before committing to them as your snack choice."

"Yeah." Quinn stuck out her tongue at her dad playfully. "What she said."

Ethan shook his head with a laugh but let it go.

I watched as she took a bite of the cookie.

Her eyes rolled back in her head, and she groaned dramatically. "These are amazing. Forget the movie. I just want to eat cookies."

"No deal." Ethan snatched up the box and stashed it behind the bar. "I've been looking forward to *Barbie* all day."

I raised my eyebrows.

"You have not," Quinn said. "But it's *so* good."

"It is good," I backed her up. "I think you'll like it, Ethan."

He shot me a look, and it was my turn to stick out my tongue at him.

"Are you coming tonight, bookstore lady?"

"It's Delaney."

"I know," Quinn told her father before grinning at me.

I winked.

I liked that she had a nickname for me. And Quinn seemed to enjoy how it made her dad a little crazy.

For a twelve-year-old, that was probably a big win.

"If you know," Ethan reprimanded, "you should use it."

"Anyway," Quinn said, ignoring him. "Are you coming tonight?"

"To movie night?"

The question took me off guard. Ethan had explained how movie night was their special father-daughter activity. He didn't have to come right out and say it for me to see how special it was to him. And considering I was just supposed to be his neighbor and friend and nothing more...

"I don't think—"

"That's very nice—"

Ethan and I spoke at the same time.

Quinn raised her eyebrows and looked between us.

I cleared my throat and spoke first. "Thanks for the invite, Quinn. That's sweet. But my night is totally booked already."

"It is?" Ethan stared at me.

Again, Quinn gave us each a look.

I focused on her before I could think too much more about it. "It is," I told her. "I need to start dragging all my Christmas decorations out of storage so I can start putting them up."

She perked up. "Like in the store?"

I nodded. "You bet."

"The *whole* store?"

"Every single corner." I smiled. "Lights, pine boughs, a window display, and...well, basically everything you can think of."

"Candy canes?"

"Obviously."

"Gingerbread houses?"

"Of course."

"A tree?"

I just gave her a "duh" look.

"What about—"

"Isn't it a little early for Christmas decorations?"

Both Quinn and I spun and stared in abject horror at her father.

"Early?"

"Never."

We both laughed, and he shook his head.

"I love Christmas," I said when I'd recovered enough. "And to be honest, it's the biggest sales season for me. I feel like I show enough restraint waiting until the start of November, to be honest."

"Fair enough." Ethan shrugged. "Maybe I should do a festive brew?"

"You totally should, Dad. Maybe a candy cane flavor."

Ethan's eyes grew wide, and he shook his head. "I should be glad you don't know anything about beer at your age, kiddo. But...no. That would be horrible."

"Whatever. I think it would be good."

I tried not to laugh. They really did have the cutest dynamic.

"I'm so jealous that you're decorating so early," Quinn said to me. "Dad won't let us put up decorations until December first."

"At the earliest," Ethan said.

"You could help me, if you like?" I extended the invitation without a second thought. "It'll be fun. We can put carols on and everything."

"Really?" Quinn jumped up from her stool. "Yes. Please. Can I, Dad?"

Ethan leaned back on the bar, looking between us. "I mean, only if I can help, too."

Quinn blinked at her father as if she didn't recognize him. "You want to decorate for Christmas? Like voluntarily?"

He shrugged. "Someone needs to hang the lights from the ceiling."

I swallowed back the urge to let him know that I'd been able to do that just fine on my own for years. Truthfully, having them both help me decorate would be fun.

The look Quinn gave her father was equal parts suspicious and surprised. "You hate all the twinkling lights."

"I never said I *hated* them," he said. "Besides, maybe I've evolved."

Quinn looked at me again, and then back at her father, as if trying to work out a problem. Finally, she shrugged. "Okay, but I get to put the angel on the tree."

"Deal." I smiled. "Only it's a star, made from old book pages."

She clapped in delight and gave me an impulsive hug.

I squeezed my eyes shut against the wave of emotions

that took me off guard and hit too hard, because this was starting to feel dangerously close to something that could be very real.

Ethan

"So what's up with you and bookstore lady?"

I almost choked on a piece of chocolate chip, salted caramel cookie, but somehow managed to recover.

"Delaney," I corrected Quinn, careful to keep my voice even.

"That's what I said." She rolled her eyes and tucked her legs up under her on the couch. On the screen, there was some sort of dance number about how Ken was enough that I pretended I was deeply interested in. "So," she said, pushing the issue. "What's the deal with you two?"

I sighed and sat back on the couch. I knew my daughter well enough to know when she wasn't going to let something go. Truthfully, I was surprised it had taken her so long to bring it up. I hadn't missed the suspicious looks she'd been giving Delaney and me at the brewery earlier.

"There's no deal."

"I thought we didn't lie to each other."

I blinked. It wasn't technically a lie. Truthfully, Delaney and I hadn't discussed what it was between the two of us.

Still, my daughter was sharp.

"It's not a lie," I answered truthfully.

Not surprisingly, Quinn wasn't satisfied with the answer. I couldn't blame her.

"Dad," she groaned and sat up, twisting her body away from the screen so she faced me head-on. "I'm not a little kid anymore. You can tell me what's going on." Before I could say anything else, she continued. "And I'm not one of those kids who're secretly hoping their parents get back together so they can have a big, happy family Christmas or something."

"You're not?" I grinned.

Quinn tossed a pillow in my direction. "You know I'm not, Dad." Her voice dropped when she added, "I know you and Mom…well, I see how different it is now."

Something about the tone in her voice stopped me. "You do?"

She nodded. "You're a lot happier in Trickle Creek. You smile more."

"I do?"

"And you laugh a lot." Quinn nodded again. "With Delaney."

Her observation, and the fact that she used Delaney's name, took me off guard. But she wasn't wrong. I *did* smile and laugh a lot with Delaney.

Before I could contribute to the conversation, Quinn continued. "Which is why I want to know what's going on between you guys. Are you dating?"

I choked on my soda.

"You like her."

"Is that a question?"

She shrugged.

I took a moment to gather my thoughts. Quinn was only twelve. But in so many ways, she was mature for her age. She'd been through so much already. She'd lost more than she even knew. And she'd just asked me a question that meant way more than it sounded.

She deserved the truth.

I inhaled a deep breath. "Yeah," I answered honestly. "I do."

She nodded and pulled her blanket up under her chin. "Good," she said. "I do, too."

I waited for her to elaborate, but she simply turned back to the movie. For a few minutes, we were both lost in the drama playing out between Barbie and Ken on the screen.

Quinn and Delaney were right. It was a pretty good movie. Not that I was ready to admit it. Especially considering I was no longer paying any attention to it. Instead, my conversation with Quinn replayed over and over in my head.

Finally, I turned to her. "You like Delaney, too?"

Quinn blew out an exasperated breath, but she was smiling when she turned to me. "You know I do. She's not fake, like a lot of grown-ups. She actually listens to me, and she recommends really good books."

I didn't bother to hide my smile.

"That and the cookies, of course." She reached for the container. Against my better judgment, I let her take another. "It was nice of her to make those for you." She wiggled her eyebrows and gave me a look that was definitely too old for her.

"What are you trying to say?"

Quinn shrugged and took a big bite of the cookie. "I don't know anyone else making you cookies just 'cause."

Fair enough.

"Look," I said after a moment. "You know that you and me…we're a team."

She nodded.

"And I really value that, Quinn." I had to tread carefully. If I got too serious with it, she'd shut down. "So I want to make sure I keep you in the loop, just like always."

"Like telling me all the things?"

I shook my head. "Age-appropriate honesty, remember?"

She groaned, and I chuckled. It was something I'd started saying to her when Polly and I were in the thick of things with our divorce. Quinn wanted to know what was going on, and I'd promised to never lie to her. But I'd also prefaced that by letting her know I'd give her one hundred percent age-appropriate honesty and some things she wasn't old enough to know yet.

She hadn't been thrilled by the idea, but she'd accepted it.

"And the truth is, I didn't tell you what was going on with Delaney right away, because I wasn't sure myself and I didn't want to confuse you or get your hopes up that—"

"But you like her?"

I nodded.

"She likes you." I tilted my head in question, but she only rolled her eyes. "You know she does, Dad."

Okay. Fair.

"You're allowed to like someone," Quinn said. "But maybe don't overthink it so much, okay? And really, let's not pretend I'm some stupid little kid who can't see what's in front of my face." She shot me a look.

"Deal."

She smiled and turned back toward the screen again.

"I knew it," she muttered under her breath.

"What's that?"

"Dad! Watch the movie. This is a good part."

Chapter Fifteen

Delaney

There were more boxes than I remembered. But then again, I had a habit of collecting decorations every year.

I stood with my hands on my hips, assessing the situation and wondering where to start when the door opened. Ethan and Quinn tumbled inside, along with a gust of cool November air.

"Did you start yet?" Quinn shrugged out of her jacket and dropped it on the floor. "Dad took *forever*. I told him we were going to be—"

"You're right on time." I grinned at her. "In fact, I haven't even picked a Christmas carol playlist yet. Do you have one?"

Her eyes lit up. "I don't. But I'll find one."

I pointed to the back of the store where I had a Bluetooth speaker. "You're in charge then. Set the mood."

Quinn didn't have to be asked twice. As soon as she took off in search of the speaker, I turned to Ethan.

"Sorry." He bent to grab his daughter's wet coat from the floor and hung it on the coat tree by the door, along with his own. "I'd say that she was raised by wolves, but that doesn't speak well for me."

He moved closer, but stopped inches from me. I yearned to reach for him and pull him in for the kiss I'd been thinking about for the last few days.

He leaned in slightly, his voice low. "Hi."

It was stupid how that one little word could make my pulse jump.

"Hi," I whispered back, biting my lower lip.

His hand brushed mine, and I sucked in a breath. He leaned in, not quite kissing me, but closer than we'd been in days.

"I've been thinking about this."

"Me too," I said softly, already closing the gap between us.

"Found it!"

Quinn's voice broke through the moment, as the first few notes of "Rockin' Around the Christmas Tree" blasted through the speaker.

We sprang apart like teenagers caught out.

Quinn appeared a second later, phone in hand. "What are—ugh." She gave us both a look that was far too knowing for a girl her age. "You two are *so* bad at this."

"Bad at what?" I put a bright smile on my face and took a step back, but she clearly didn't buy it.

"Don't worry," she said. "I already told Dad I was cool with it."

I blinked and glanced at Ethan. "Told him what?"

"That I know." She gave me a "duh" look. "About you two." Quinn laughed. "You two aren't exactly subtle."

I was at a loss for words. Ethan scratched the back of his neck, doing a terrible job at hiding his smile.

I stared at Quinn, trying and failing to come up with something, anything. "Oh."

Quinn shrugged and started to dig into a nearby box as if nothing of interest had just happened.

I looked at Ethan with wide, questioning eyes, but he only shrugged. "She's cool with it."

"With *it*?"

We still hadn't talked about what *it* was.

"Can you guys just not be gross about it, please?"

"Gross?" I was starting to feel like a broken record.

"Yeah." Quinn pulled a tangle of mini lights from a box. "Like kissing and stuff."

Next to me, Ethan burst out laughing. His daughter shot him a look, and he very quickly stifled his laughter. "Deal," he said as seriously as possible. "We'll keep things G-rated."

"Good." She went back to digging through the box as if she hadn't just completely thrown me for a loop I hadn't seen coming.

Of course, I'd never dated a man with a child before. If that even *was* what we were doing. I blinked a few times and shook my head before I turned back to the stack of boxes, pretending to take inventory while I took a few minutes to collect myself.

I shouldn't have been surprised that Quinn had noticed something between us. Maybe even before we did. She was a smart, observant kid. Still, hearing her say it out loud, like it was no big deal—when it in fact was a very big deal—left me feeling a little unsettled.

Not in a bad way.

Just in a different, I have no idea how to act, kind of way.

"Bookstore lady." Quinn's use of my nickname jarred me from my overthinking and just like that, it felt normal again. I turned to see her holding up a handful of ornaments. "Are these for the tree?"

"They sure are."

I turned again when Ethan spoke. "Where are you going to put all these lights, Delaney?" Ethan lifted a bundle from one of the boxes. "You have enough in here to light up the entire plaza."

I gestured toward the windows. "Start there, and work your way through the store," I told him. "I put them along all the shelves, the ceiling, the railing over there, and—"

"Everything," Ethan finished for me.

"Now you're getting it." I winked at him and went to join Quinn, who had started to unbox the ornaments for the tree.

"These are the cutest little books," she exclaimed, holding up one of my favorite ornaments.

I smiled at her and reached for another.

I knew I could have done it on my own, the way I had in the past, but standing there, laughing with Quinn like it was the most natural thing in the world, while Ethan struggled with way too many strands of lights, trying not to curse out loud…

That was better.

A lot better.

Ethan

It's not that I didn't like Christmas. I did.

In December. For two days.

I'd never been the type of person to drag out the holiday season for an entire month, let alone for *two* whole months.

When Quinn was little, I worked hard to make the holidays special for her. Especially because Polly was always too busy to do the traditional things like decorating the tree or making a gingerbread house.

She always had a string of excuses as to why she couldn't fit the special family time into her schedule. I remember getting into big arguments early on about how she needed to adjust her priorities, but over time, I simply lost the energy for the fight.

It wasn't like she was ever going to change. In hindsight, it was probably all those years of arguing and trying to convince Polly to participate that tainted the holiday season for me a little bit.

Which was why I didn't expect to enjoy decorating Delaney's shop so much. Especially in early November, which—despite how much fun I'd actually had with Quinn and Delaney—I still thought was *way* too early to decorate.

But truthfully, it didn't take long before I kind of got into it.

Okay, I got *a lot* into it.

Maybe it was the music that Quinn found. The perfect mix of holiday classics and fun, upbeat versions I'd never heard before. Maybe it was the pine and spice candle Delaney had lit at the front of the shop.

But more likely, it was Delaney herself.

And the way she had Quinn laughing and forgetting that as an almost teenager, it probably wasn't *cool* to have so much fun decorating a Christmas tree and hanging garland.

Watching the way the two of them interacted so easily stopped me more than once. Their easy laughter and playful jabs back and forth looked like the most natural thing in the world.

The way a family should be.

The thought stopped me cold. It was *way* too early for me to be having such thoughts. We'd only just started... whatever it was we were doing. Quinn wasn't even used to the idea of Delaney and I together, let alone the two of us having a moment to get used to it.

Or even discuss it properly.

Still.

Maybe it wouldn't hurt to let myself fantasize about what *could* be.

Delaney was untangling yet another strand of fairy lights while Quinn attempted to assemble some sort of snowman on a nearby bookshelf. I didn't want to say anything, but I was pretty sure she had the snowballs in the wrong order.

When it fell over for the second time, she grabbed the decoration and tossed it back in the box. "I need cookies," she announced. "This is important festive work and I require snacks."

"There's a tray upstairs," Delaney said over her shoulder. "I set out everything for hot chocolate, too. Just hit the power button on the kettle and heat up the water."

"Seriously?"

"Of course." Delaney turned. "You don't really think I would expect us to decorate without Christmas goodies, do you?"

In response, Quinn laughed and took off upstairs in search of the snacks without another word.

The second she disappeared up the back staircase, Delaney turned toward me, a smile pulling at her lips. "Are you hating every minute of this?"

I shook my head and descended the ladder. "Not at all," I answered honestly. "I'm actually enjoying it." I lifted a hand toward the box that, despite my best efforts, was still full of lights waiting to be hung. "But I still think you have way too many lights."

She threw back her head in laughter. "Never." And as if to prove her point, she held out the lights she'd just untangled and spun in a quick circle, wrapping herself up like a present I would very much like to unwrap.

"I should plug you in and light you up." I reached for her cheek.

"Ethan." She pretended to be shocked. "You're such a dirty talker."

This time, when she giggled, I cut her off with a deep kiss.

With her lips pressed to mine, her laughter dissolved into a groan that sent a shot of heat right between my legs and made my dick twitch with the need to get her alone.

"Mmm." She touched her finger to her lips as I stepped back. "You lit me up, all right."

More than anything, I wanted to continue exactly what we'd started and forget all about the stack of boxes and mess around us. But I was all too aware that Quinn was just upstairs and acting on my impulses would definitely fall way out of the G-rated boundaries she'd set.

"You didn't tell me that Quinn knew about…well…*us*," Delaney said, her thoughts obviously drifting to a similar place.

"Is that okay?"

"Of course it is." She didn't hesitate. "I hated keeping it from her as long as we did."

"Which wasn't very long."

She chuckled. "No. It wasn't."

"It turns out that we're not very good actors." I reached for her again, my hand finding her waist through the strings of lights. I pulled her close, unable to keep away from her.

"So?" she asked before I could kiss her again. "What did you tell her? What exactly is this between us?"

I hesitated, but only for a second. "I don't know," I answered honestly. "But it feels good." I pressed a kiss to her forehead. "Really good."

"It does." Her smile was soft. "It feels real."

"It sure does." I pulled her closer.

"We probably shouldn't be having this discussion in what looks to be a snow globe explosion."

I shook my head. "I think this is a conversation best left for later." I kissed her nose. "When we're alone."

"Mmm."

Our lips met again in another deep kiss that made me long for more. I shifted her light-wrapped body so I could hold her closer and deepen our connection, when—

"Come *on*," Quinn groaned from behind me. "I thought we agreed to no gross stuff."

Reluctantly, I pulled away from Delaney, but kept my hand on her hip.

"Did you find the cookies?" Delaney's voice was casual, as if she wasn't currently wrapped up like a present I'd been seconds away from unwrapping.

"I did." Quinn gave her a strange look as she walked past with the loaded tray. "And I mixed up three cups of hot chocolate. Extra marshmallows."

"Just the way I like it."

Quinn set the tray on the top of Delaney's rickety front counter and the whole structure swayed dangerously.

I reached out quickly to steady it. "I thought you were going to get this looked at?" I dropped into a crouch and grabbed the block she used to keep it level. It had been knocked loose. Again. "I got it." I stood and dusted my hands on my pant legs. "But it's not a permanent solution."

"I know." Delaney spun herself around, untangling herself from the lights. "It's on the list of things I need to get to," she said. "After Christmas." She winked. "I've been a little busy."

"You know I can help if you—"

"I got it, Ethan." She stopped me gently. "Truthfully, I don't want to bother fixing it if I can. Instead, I've been keeping my eye out for something to replace it. I just haven't found the right thing yet. This was always supposed to be a temporary counter anyway. Maybe after the holiday season…"

Before I could push any further, Quinn thrust a cookie between us.

"This is *so* good. Dad, you have to try these."

Delaney turned away as I took the cookie from Quinn.

"Gingerbread," I said as I took a bite. "How do you have Christmas cookies already?" I raised my eyebrows. "I mean, it's one thing to decorate way too early, but cookies? Don't tell me you were baking all night."

"Okay, I won't tell you that." Delaney laughed. "But only because I wasn't. I froze these last season, because Quinn is one hundred percent right. You can't decorate without festive snacks."

"You have a ton," Quinn said. "It's lucky we're here to help you eat them."

"It is *very* lucky." Delaney looked over Quinn's head, a small smile on her face. "I guess we have your dad to thank for opening a brewery right next door."

I raised an eyebrow at her. "You're thanking me for that now, are you?"

She shrugged. "Well…maybe I'm not *thanking* you for it. But…"

"Whatever! It's still lucky." Quinn laughed and raised a mug of hot chocolate in the air. "Cheers to cookies."

"Cheers to cookies," we both dutifully repeated.

Delaney

It took a few more hours of work to get everything in the boxes out and on display. I still had the front window display of a Christmas tree made out of books to put together, but that would have to wait.

Long after the cookies were gone and Quinn and Ethan had gone home, I surveyed my festive shop with a smile. I always loved it when the decorations went up, but it felt different this time. Special.

And as I flicked off the lights and headed up to bed myself, Quinn's words from earlier rang in my ears, and I couldn't help but think about exactly how lucky I was.

Chapter Sixteen

Delaney

"Why do we insist on having our girls' night the same night they do trivia?" I asked, as Lauren and I pushed our way through the crowd to get to the table Kat came early to save for us. "It's *so* busy in here."

Lauren laughed. "Because trivia is fun, obviously."

I shot her a look as we both slid into our seats. Me across from Kat, who already had one of the Wildflower's fancy mocktails in front of her, and Lauren across from Avery, who looked like she'd also just arrived.

"When was the last time we did actual trivia at trivia night?" I directed the question to Avery.

"Careful." Kat grinned. "That sounds like a trivia question."

I groaned and reached for a menu.

"I'm just happy to get away from the inn for a few hours," Avery said. "Don't get me wrong. I love it and all, but…"

"I get it." Lauren nodded. "Running your own business is satisfying and rewarding and blah blah blah. But also…"

"It's *so* good to have a break," Kat chimed in. "And double so to get a break from mom life, too. Don't get me wrong, baby Billy is amazing, but some time off from everything is great, too. Trivia night or not."

"I will cheers to that," I said. "As soon as I get a glass of wine."

As if by magic, the server chose that moment to appear with a tray full of drinks.

"She's super busy," Kat said. "So I took a chance and got everyone their usual."

"You are the best." Lauren blew her a kiss.

A minute later, we all had drinks in hand and were able to properly toast to a night off from any responsibilities.

"I can't believe you're all decorated for the holiday already." Avery put her glass down and stared at me. "I'm still trying to decide what to do at the inn, and Reid said you were all finished?"

"It's true." I shrugged. "I just really like Christmas. I always do it as early as I can get away with."

"And this year you had a little extra help." Avery wiggled her eyebrows.

I blushed and ducked my head.

"Care to tell us about that?"

All three women stared at me, waiting for the gossip. I pretended to be engrossed in the menu for a moment before Kat snatched it from my hand. "I already ordered us a charcuterie board, Delaney. Now, spill."

"Spill?"

"You and the sexy brewmaster," she said. "Have you guys made it official yet?"

I glanced at Lauren for help, but she simply shrugged.

"Yes," I confessed. "Ethan and I are dating."

It was the first time I said it out loud. It felt good.

Kat squealed. Lauren clapped and Avery just grinned.

"It's about time," Lauren said. "I didn't think the two of you were ever going to get over the whole next-door enemies thing."

"We weren't really *enemies*…"

"Right…" She dragged out the word. "You just hated the fact that a smooth-talking charmer with too much dust and noise and a brewery had moved in next door to your peaceful little bookshop."

"Okay, maybe we were sort of enemies." I laughed. "But that was before."

"Before you realized he was a sexy piece of—"

"Before," I cut Kat off smoothly, "Ethan showed me how considerate he could be with my shop and…well, truth-fully, before I got to know him."

"And his sexy ass." Kat couldn't help herself, and we all laughed.

"Honestly," I said after a moment. "There are still a few noise issues during my cozy mystery book club and my writing group. But beyond that, he's been a really respectful neighbor and…yes, now that we've gotten to know each other, well…let's just say…things are good."

The server returned with a huge platter that she set in the middle of the table. For a few minutes, we were all quiet, distracted by cheese and meat.

"Okay." Kat held up a cracker stacked with brie and salami. "I think we're all dying to hear some details."

There was no hiding the blush on my face. "Details?"

"Well, maybe not *details*," Lauren said, and I shot her a grateful look. "But…"

It was clear that my girlfriends weren't going to let it go

without me telling them *something*. With a sigh, I picked a grape off the board and popped it into my mouth.

Ethan

"You sure you want another round?" Brody asked, already waving down the server before I could answer. "Because I can't be held responsible for you if you have too many." He was laughing, but I still jabbed him in the ribs with my elbow.

"Right." I rolled my eyes. "Because *I'm* the lightweight in the family."

"Nope," Reid jumped in. "That honor goes to our little brother. Always has."

Preston wasn't offended. Instead, he held up his glass of water, grinning. "Don't be a hater just because I care about my body."

"Right, you care so much about your body that you throw it off cliffs and hurtle down mountains at ridiculous speeds." Grayson raised an eyebrow before taking another sip of his drink.

It was true. Our youngest brother was an adrenaline junkie and had been since we were little. It never failed to stress out our mother, who'd rather not hear about what latest adventures Preston got up to. But the rest of us had gotten used to hearing about his hijinks. And considering he worked with the local search and rescue, we trusted that he was smart enough to know what he was doing and not get hurt.

"Whatever." Brody thanked the waitress who delivered a fresh round of drinks. "I still remember that one time I had to carry you up to your room, little brother."

"I was seventeen." Preston shook his head.

"And you'll never live it down."

The Brickhouse pub was loud, the wings were hot, and the beer was cold—even if it wasn't my brew. Some time with my brothers just to unwind and shoot the shit was the perfect way to let go of the stress of a long week. It was long overdue.

"Speaking of things you're never going to live down..." Grayson shifted in his chair and eyed me.

I knew what was coming. My brothers weren't the type to stay quiet about...well, anything. Especially when it came to our love lives.

We'd all tried and failed when it came to Reid and his fake marriage to Avery, which turned out to be real. I couldn't imagine any of my brothers were going to keep their mouths shut about Delaney and me.

Still, it was fun to fuck with them a little. Or at least make them work for it.

I lifted the glass to my mouth and smirked. "What are you talking about?"

Grayson groaned. "Are you going to tell us what's going on with you and Delaney, or do we all have to keep pretending that we don't notice the way you both look at each other?"

"There's not much to say."

Brody looked over his pint glass and raised his eyebrows. "And...that's a lie."

"If you're not going to tell them, I will," Reid chimed in.

"Oh yeah? You think you know something?"

My brother laughed. "I know that Quinn couldn't stop talking about the two of you at our ice cream date the other day and how *gross* you both are."

Busted.

Reid's twin, Grayson, laughed. "Gotta love that kid. She won't let anyone get away with anything."

"Least of all me." I shook my head, but I couldn't help but chuckle. It was true. My girl was sharp. Nothing got by her. Delaney and I were proof of that.

"Okay," Preston jumped in. "We all agree that Quinn is the coolest kid ever and the very best thing you've ever done."

I rolled my eyes.

"But what I think we all really want to know is what is going on with you and Delaney? And why does Quinn think it's gross?"

"I have no doubt that Ethan is gross," Brody jumped in. "But Delaney is—"

"Careful." I held up a hand to stop him, and my brother gave me a shit-eating grin. "Fine." It was clear I wasn't going to be able to finish my hot wings in peace if I didn't give them something. "As you've all obviously figured out, Delaney and I are dating."

"It's official then?"

I nodded at Reid and couldn't help but smile because that woman put a smile on my face, even when she wasn't around. I probably hadn't stopped smiling for longer than thirty seconds since the night of the snowstorm.

"I like her," I said, more serious than I intended. "A lot. She's smart, gorgeous, and doesn't let me get away with anything."

"Oh, that is serious." Grayson snagged another wing off the tray. "Seriously," he added. "You sound happy."

I didn't say anything for a minute, because admitting it out loud felt almost like tempting fate. Like if I admitted how good it felt to be with Delaney, how natural and easy it was, it would all go away, or I'd find a way to mess it up.

Eventually, I simply said, "I am."

Brody nodded, the teasing fading a little. "Good. You deserve it, Ethan."

"Thanks. That means a lot." I lifted my glass in his direction before taking a deep drink.

Delaney

"What can I say? It's been nice."

"Nice?"

I nodded. "I know it's not super exciting and dramatic. But does it have to be?"

"You tell us," Avery said. "You're the expert on happily ever afters." She winked, and I laughed.

"Just because I like to read them doesn't mean I'm an expert on anything," I assured her. "In fact, quite the opposite. But..." I let my thoughts drift away. "This thing with Ethan is different, and I think that's in part because it's not full of drama. It's just easy. Being with him feels really natural."

"I love that." Lauren gave me a warm smile. "That's how it should be."

"Oh?" Kat raised her eyebrow. "Is that how it is with you and Brody?"

My mouth dropped open at Kat's boldness. Not that I should be surprised. Kat was never afraid to ask the questions we were all thinking. Still, I wanted to hear the answer just as much as anyone.

"We're not talking about me and Brody," Lauren answered smoothly.

"But there is something to talk about?"

Lauren gave Kat a look before turning her back on her and getting back to the topic at hand. "I'm glad it's going so well with Ethan," she said. "What about Quinn? How's she with it all?"

I smiled. "She's great and way too smart."

"She figured it out first, didn't she?" Avery grinned when I nodded.

"She did."

"She might have mentioned something the night of the snowstorm about how the two of you were getting closer," Avery said.

That didn't surprise me at all.

"So she's okay with everything?" Lauren plucked a block of cheese from the tray. "That's good."

"It is." I nodded. "She's fine as long as we keep things *G-rated*." I used air quotes. "She doesn't want to see any *gross* stuff."

"But the gross stuff is the best part." Kat laughed.

I couldn't deny that. I'd definitely been enjoying the very not G-rated things Ethan and I had been doing whenever we had a little bit of alone time. Which wasn't nearly as often as I would have liked, but was completely understandable.

"And how do you feel about the whole *bonus mom* thing, Delaney?"

Avery's question caught me off guard. "Bonus mom?"

"You know," she explained. "You're not her mom, because she has one of those." The statement hung in the air because we both knew how absent Quinn's actual mother was. "But you're like a *bonus*."

"Huh." I sat with that for a moment.

"It's not a small thing," Lauren said. "A while ago, I dated a man with kids. It brings a whole other element to the relationship. Like, it's not just the two of you to consider."

I opened my mouth but closed it again, because she was right. Truthfully, I just hadn't let myself go there yet. Not in all the moments we'd shared together in the bookstore and the brewery. Or even those times where Quinn would tell a joke or say something sarcastic that might push the limits a little, only to look at me to see how I'd react.

"You know," Kat said, "you might want to talk to my sister-in-law, Lucy, about it. Their situation is a little different in that Lucy was technically Meri's nanny before she and Craig hooked up. But, she had to settle right into that mother role, too. She might have some words of wisdom for you."

I nodded. That wasn't a bad idea.

"I'm not trying to be her mom," I said, choosing my words carefully. "I'm not trying to...well, I'm not sure what I'm trying to do yet."

"It's still early days." Lauren offered me a small smile.

I smiled in return before stuffing my mouth with a cracker full of cheddar and fig jam. But even as the conversation turned to Kat, Andy, and the baby, a quiet part of me couldn't let go of the conversation or the new and unexpected questions it had brought up.

Ethan

"I forgot what mediocre beer tastes like." I winked and reached for the pitcher the server had placed on the table.

"Not all beer can be fancy craft beer, brother."

"Nor should it be," Reid agreed with his twin.

"How is it going with the brewery, anyway?" Brody asked. "You still thinking about doing a patio expansion?"

Truthfully, the idea of a patio had been put on the back burner almost as immediately as it had come up when

Brody had mentioned it. I was busy enough with the day-to-day running of the brewery.

Some days, it was all I could do to keep my head above water with managing inventory, production, operations, and then of course there was the whole human resources part of things. I'd been pretty lucky so far with the staff I'd hired, but managing people came with a whole different type of stress I hadn't considered before.

I shook my head and lifted the glass to my lips again. "Honestly? It's been chaos."

"Especially now that you're juggling a new relationship along with everything else," Brody said. "That's never easy."

"Because you're one to know." Preston elbowed him in the ribs. "When was the last time you were in a relationship? And hookups don't count."

We all stared at our oldest brother, who choked on his beer before finally wiping his mouth on the back of his hand. "All I'm saying is, it's a lot."

It was an interesting cop-out, especially since we'd all been wondering for years what exactly was going on between Brody and Lauren. But it didn't take a detective to see we weren't any closer to getting any information out of him this time either.

"Anyway." Reid exaggerated the word, his eyes wide as he looked at me. "Back to the patio idea. It's a good one."

"Putting a few tables out front would be pretty sweet," Preston said. "With those big garage door windows open, it would be like an inside-outside situation."

"That's smart," Reid said. "A few heaters for the shoulder season, and some big planter baskets…maybe some string lights."

"String lights?" Brody eyed him sideways. "Who are you right now?"

Reid shrugged. "What can I say? Avery's shown me the way when it comes to string lights. It really does make a space cozy."

We all stared at our grumpy, turned soft and gooey, brother and shook our heads before I pulled the conversation back.

"He's not wrong," I conceded. "And really, a few planters and strings of lights would be a hell of a lot easier than trying to transform the back-alley space right now."

"Good point." Grayson pointed at me with a chicken wing. "No construction and minimal overhead."

I nodded. "There's only one problem."

"Oh yeah."

"Good point."

"Right."

"Delaney."

I stared at my brothers. "What? Delaney?"

They all nodded.

"What were you thinking the problem was?" Grayson asked.

"The town," I said slowly. "Getting a permit to add tables into the plaza and expand my liquor license."

"Oh." Brody pretended to consider that for a moment. "Yeah, no. That's not going to be a problem. The town is all about encouraging business and foot traffic in the plaza. I bet you take it to the next town hall meeting and it's approved before you walk out."

"Really?"

"Totally." Brody shrugged. "I've been going to those meetings long enough to know how they'll turn out. I doubt it'll be a problem."

"I agree," Reid said. "The town's been pushing for more community spaces and outdoor seating. This fits that vibe."

I grabbed another wing and dipped it into the ranch before taking a bite while I let myself really think about the possibility of a front patio space for the first time. I had to admit, the additional tables would be great for business, and there was nothing better than enjoying a cold beer on a patio in the summer sun.

"Yes," I said aloud. "I think this will be good. Low investment, big payoff." I let the smile cross my face. "Let's do it."

"And by let's…" Reid shot me a look, and I laughed.

"Don't worry, brother," I told him. "I know you're busy. I don't think this project will require too much in the way of construction. I might even be able to handle it on my own."

It was Brody's turn to laugh. "Yeah, right. You know we'll help out."

The conversation drifted away from the brewery and expansion plans into talk about sports and whatever new adventure Preston had just signed up for, and it wasn't long before I'd completely forgotten all about what the real concern regarding the brewery's patio should have been.

Chapter Seventeen

Delaney

"You know this is a bold choice, right?" Ethan handed me a mug of hot chocolate.

At least, I assumed it was hot chocolate. There was so much whipped cream on the top that I couldn't really tell what was underneath it all.

"How so?" I raised an eyebrow and reached for the tray of hot chocolate toppings.

"You went full classic." Ethan grinned as he sat next to me on the couch. His thigh pressed up against mine in a way that sent sparks flying through me, and made me wiggle a little bit closer. "Not just an *old* classic, but a really old classic. Quinn thinks the nineties were old and the eighties were ancient."

I sprinkled chocolate chips on the top of my drink. "That's a problem?" For the first time, I was genuinely concerned that maybe I'd not chosen my very first movie night selection well. As soon as I'd received the invite from Quinn, the day before when she burst through the door of

Plot Twist with a grin and more of a demand that I attend, rather than an invitation, I knew exactly what movie I wanted to bring.

"She's a teenager." Ethan raised an eyebrow. "Teens are a fickle bunch."

"She's not a teenager yet." I laughed. "We still have a few months before we need to face that particular battle."

We.

"Besides," I continued as if I hadn't just casually referenced the fact that I hoped to be around and involved for Quinn's *troubling teen* years. "She's going to love *Gone with the Wind*. I think she may even find a kindred spirit in Scarlett."

"I wouldn't know." Ethan shrugged. "I've never seen it."

My mouth fell open, and I sat back on the couch, rethinking all of my life choices. "Seriously?"

He nodded.

"I don't know if I can date you," I joked as Quinn joined us with a mug in hand and the biggest bowl of popcorn I'd ever seen.

"Are you breaking up with him already?" She plopped down on the other side of me. "Is it because he didn't use enough whipped cream? I told him it wasn't enough."

With a raised eyebrow, I glanced from my overflowing mug to Quinn's, which somehow had even more whipped cream spilling over the top.

"No, the whipped cream is fine." I shook my head. "He's never seen *Gone with the Wind*," I told her. "It's a classic."

"Isn't that what we're watching tonight?"

"It is."

"Then we'll all be caught up," Quinn told me. "And you can keep him around a bit longer." She elbowed me gently. "Even if he is a little cheap on the whipped cream."

We both laughed, but Ethan just groaned and reached

for the remote control. "Okay, that's enough. Let's get to the movie before we make any big decisions."

"Good point." Quinn turned to me. "I hope it's not too boring," she said. "Because if it is, you're banned from choosing for like…what? A year, Dad?"

"At least," Ethan agreed with a grin.

"Deal," I said, even though I already knew she was going to love it. She was way too smart not to.

The opening credits rolled, and the three of us settled in. Ethan's arm stretched behind me on the couch, his fingers dangling over my shoulder like he was trying not to touch me, lest Quinn think it was gross, but still wanted to be close. Quinn tucked her feet up under her and leaned her head against my shoulder like it was the most natural thing in the world.

Like the three of us were the most natural thing.

And maybe we were.

My thoughts flitted back to the conversation I'd had with my friends a few nights earlier. I wasn't trying to be her mom. I was just trying to be *there*.

More importantly, I *wanted* to be there.

That meant something.

Ethan

I rinsed the last of the hot chocolate mugs and handed them to Delaney, who stood at the ready with a dish towel. Behind me, the dishwasher hummed quietly with the rest of our dishes. Almost as soon as the end credits rolled, Quinn had slipped away to her room under the pretense of being exhausted and far too tired to be able to help clean up.

I didn't press the issue the way I normally would have, eager to spend even a few moments alone with Delaney.

Movie night had been fun, but I was more than ready for a little PG-13 rated time. At *least*.

"She liked it," I said, breaking the easy silence between us.

Delaney looked up. "Quinn?"

I nodded, and she smiled.

"I knew she would," Delaney said with a grin. "It might be an oldie, but I thought she might connect with Scarlett."

"You were right." I took the dry mug from her hand and put it in the cupboard. "She said it was old but pretty cool for a *super classic*. And I'd say that's pretty high praise coming from a twelve-year-old. Good job on your first pick."

"I'm just glad I didn't get banned. Besides, now that you've seen it, I guess I can keep you."

"Oh yeah?" I leaned back against the counter. "You think so?"

"Hmm." She stepped closer, the dish towel still in her hand. "Should I make you give me a movie report?"

I raised my brow in question.

"It's like a book report, only for a movie."

"Gotcha." I reached for her hip and pulled her close. "Well, let's see...a feisty heroine, old-school romance. Big grand gestures and goodbyes that aren't goodbyes. How did I do?"

She pressed up against me, her lips only inches from mine. "Pretty good."

I closed the space between us and kissed her until she groaned into my mouth.

"That was pretty good, too," she said after a moment.

"I can do a whole lot better than *pretty good*." I bent to press kisses on her neck to demonstrate my point, but she pulled away.

My body ached to have her closer. It felt like an eternity

since we'd been alone together. Besides a few stolen moments here and there, we'd hardly even kissed.

"You don't have to leave," I told her. "Not tonight."

"Ethan. I—"

"Tell me you don't want to."

"I can't," she said without hesitation. "It's just…"

"I know," I said softly. "It's a lot and it's still new and… all of that. But, the truth is, I like having you here."

"I like being here."

"So stay." I wiggled my brows.

She laughed, but in the next second, shook her head. "It's just so…"

"I know." My laughter dried up, and a soft smile crossed my face. "But this feels different, doesn't it?"

She nodded, confirming what I already knew. This thing between us was different than anything I'd ever felt before with anyone.

"If there are rules to how we're supposed to move forward, I don't know them," I continued. "And even if I did, I don't think I care."

I reached for her again, my hands gripping her hips.

"What about Quinn?"

I didn't take my eyes off her. "Her room is on the other side of the house. And, she'll be asleep by now."

"And in the morning?"

"She'll be thrilled you're still here." It was the truth.

Delaney hesitated, as if she were weighing the pros and cons in her head.

"Stay," I said softly. "Please."

She leaned in, closing the space between us with a kiss.

When we pulled apart, the look she gave me went straight to my chest. I had to suck in a breath just to steady myself before I could move again.

I took her hand, laced my fingers through hers, and led her down the hall, flipping off the lights as we passed through the quiet house.

Delaney

As Ethan closed the door with a soft click behind us, I took a moment to take in his room.

It was pretty basic, and definitely that of a single man with a simple comforter covering the bed and no throw pillows. There was a picture of Ethan and Quinn when she was little, riding on his shoulders, in a frame on the dresser. A print of a mountain landscape hung over the bed. But beyond that, there was nothing in the way of decoration.

When I turned around, Ethan was watching me, but he didn't say a word, just looked at me with a familiar hunger in his eyes.

The weight of what this was, and what it might mean to spend the night, settled over me. But I didn't want to make it into more than it was, so I cocked a hip and said, "So, do you bring all your dates to family movie night?"

He grinned and stepped closer. "Only the ones who can make classic movies seem cool. So far, there's only ever been one."

"So far?"

"I can't imagine there could ever be another."

My stomach flipped.

When he reached out to brush the hair off my face, I was totally gone.

"It's been a while," I said, my voice shaky. "Since we've been alone."

"Too long." He leaned in.

"Way too long."

The kiss started slow, but it didn't stay that way for long. My hands were on his chest, then under his shirt, and then it was coming off and over his head.

His hands slid down my back until he found the hem of my sweater. I lifted my arms so he could pull it up and over my head. I reached for his in return, taking my time brushing my fingers over bare skin.

Back and forth, we took turns peeling layers of clothing off each other between charged kisses that grew more and more insistent, like we'd been waiting forever to be together again like this.

It felt like it.

He tugged me in, our mouths meeting again and his hands sliding down my back while my hands moved over his body. Together, we stumbled backward toward the bed.

"Did you lock the door?"

"Quinn's out cold."

"That's not a yes." I pulled back and gave him a look.

It already felt way too risky to be here like this—not that I wanted to leave, but we needed to be smart.

Ethan groaned, kissed me once more, and stepped away to click the door lock in place.

When he came back, he cupped my cheek and kissed me hard.

The moan that slipped from deep inside me was swallowed by his kisses until my back hit the mattress. His body followed. Warm and solid and exactly where I wanted him.

"I missed this," I said, breathless as he worked his way down my body with his lips.

He looked up with a sexy half smile. "You're not the only one, sweetheart."

His hands skimmed down my sides and over my hips, as if he were memorizing every inch of my body.

We'd done this before, but this time it felt different.

It felt like more.

Like we were finally letting ourselves have this without pretending that it didn't mean something real.

He kissed me again, slower now as I fell into it. My body shifted and arched up into him.

"I hope you're not too tired," I whispered against his mouth before biting his lower lip a little.

"Not even close," he said, his voice rough with need. "I've been thinking about this from the moment you walked in the door."

"Is that right?" My body thrummed with the promise held in his words as he slid his thick length inside me. "Then maybe you should show me exactly what you've been thinking about."

"Oh, sweetheart." He nipped the sensitive spot beneath my ear. "That's exactly what I intend to do."

He did.

And for the next little while, neither of us had much to say at all.

Ethan

I poured two cups of coffee, adding a splash of cream in one mug before turning back to the bacon sizzling on the stovetop.

Outside, the snow had stopped overnight, coating the yard on our little piece of property on the edge of town in a sparkling layer of fresh white stuff. Winter was well and truly here. A little earlier than normal, but I didn't mind.

Because inside it was cozy and warm.

Even more so when a moment later, Delaney padded into the kitchen. "Good morning."

I moved across the room to pull her in for a sleepy kiss and hand her a coffee. "Good morning to you, beautiful. I hope I didn't wake you."

"Are you kidding? Waking up to the smell of bacon and coffee is probably the best way to wake up on a Sunday." Her smile was slow and a little shy.

"I can think of a few better ways," I whispered gruffly in her ear, causing her to blush.

She swatted me away and looked down at the mug I'd handed her. "You know how I take my coffee?"

"Splash of cream," I said easily. "Of course I do."

She blinked at me and, for a moment, looked like she might say something more. Instead, she smiled and took a sip while I turned my attention back to breakfast duties.

"Scrambled or fried?" I asked, pulling the eggs from the fridge. "I was thinking cheesy scrambled."

"That sounds perfect."

While I worked, Delaney leaned up against the counter, sipping her coffee. She was wearing the same clothes as the night before, but her hair was pulled up in a sloppy bun, and she'd swapped her contacts for her glasses, giving her a very sexy librarian look that made it hard to concentrate on cooking.

"You're humming," Delaney said after a few minutes.

"I'm happy."

"You hum when you're happy?"

With the whisk in one hand, I turned to stroke her cheek and pull her in close. "It seems that I do." I gave her a quick kiss.

"Ugh. It's way too early for gross stuff."

We pulled apart with a laugh as Quinn joined us in the kitchen.

Delaney held up her hands, but I couldn't promise to

keep my hands off her. Not after the night we'd shared in my bed.

"You may have to settle for a PG rating today."

Quinn groaned again, but I didn't miss the small smile that crossed her lips.

I handed her a glass of orange juice as she slid into her seat at the table. "Cheesy scrambled?"

"Is there another kind?"

Delaney and I exchanged a glance, both of us smiling.

Damn.

I couldn't even say that I'd missed the kind of easy comfort of a Sunday morning in the kitchen because I didn't think I'd ever had it.

Everything about having Delaney in the house felt easy, like we'd been doing it forever already. Like everything was already in place.

I slid the eggs from a pan into the bowl and handed them to Delaney before plating the bacon and joining them at the table.

"This is…"

"Nice," I finished for Quinn with a raised eyebrow.

"Yeah." She shrugged. "I mean, I was gonna say cool. But I guess nice is a perfectly *okay* word, too."

Delaney laughed and reached for a piece of toast. "I agree," she said. "It's very cool." She winked at me. "And pretty nice, too."

Over the breakfast table, conversation flowed effortlessly. Quinn filled us in on some of the latest gossip among the sixth-grade class before moving into negotiations on how early was *too* early for a Christmas tree.

"Not until December."

"No fair." Quinn scowled.

"You can enjoy all of Delaney's decorations for another

month," I told her. "But no tree until at *least* December first around here."

Delaney and Quinn exchanged a glance. I got the distinct feeling that the conversation wasn't over, and I'd probably be on the losing end of whatever the two of them decided.

When we were done eating, I pushed my plate back. "You're going to be on your own for dinner tomorrow night, kiddo. I have the community meeting." I looked at Delaney. "I guess *we* have it."

"Not me." She shook her head. "I need to run out to the city and see what happened with my last holiday inventory order that was delayed. The shipping hub called and told me they received it, but the paperwork is all messed up. I need to go sort it out in person if I want my full stock in time for the holidays."

"That's a pain."

"You're telling me." Delaney grabbed the plates and took them to the sink.

"Can I come? I doubt my homework will be—"

"No," we both said at the same time. I shook my head and added, "Homework comes first. You know that."

"Besides," Delaney added. "The meetings are usually pretty boring. You're not missing much. Budget talks and maybe one or two proposal permits. Tilley Beckett will no doubt have some sort of update on whatever festival is coming up next, but..." She shrugged. "Pretty dull."

"Sounds like it." Quinn pushed away from the table and helped Delaney clean up. "But I was asking if I could come to the city."

"No deal, kiddo," I said smoothly. "You have to go to school." I exchanged smiles with Delaney. "If it's not too much trouble, though..."

She tilted her head. "What? You have errands you need me to run?"

It was pretty common when someone was making the trek to the city for them to pick up a few things for friends.

"I actually have some label samples from a new supplier that I'd love to grab. They were going to throw them in the mail, but—"

"No problem. Send me the address and I'll save you the postage. But it'll cost you." She winked, Quinn groaned again, and we all laughed.

I thought briefly about the patio proposal I'd submitted. And for a moment, I considered mentioning it to Delaney. It was on the docket for tomorrow night, but I doubted it would get much discussion. A few tables weren't going to cause much controversy. Not when there were festivals to plan. It's not like it was a big deal.

Delaney glanced over at me again, and I smiled without thinking. She smiled back and just like that, nothing else mattered. Especially not boring town meetings or permits. The only thing on my mind was Delaney and Quinn and how somehow, when I wasn't looking for it, the start of something real between all three of us had started to grow.

Something that was starting to feel more and more like a family.

Chapter Eighteen

Delaney

My trip to the city had been surprisingly smooth. I still didn't understand why the shipping hub needed to see me in person, requiring a four-hour drive both ways, but considering it got my inventory shipment released, it was time well spent.

At least, that's how I had to look at it.

And because everything went so smoothly with the shipping hub, I was able to complete my little side quest to pick up Ethan's labels quicker than expected, too.

I was still about ten minutes away from Trickle Creek when I noticed the time. The community meeting would still be underway.

I didn't have to go.

It had been a long day. What I really should do was drive straight home, make myself a mug of herbal tea, light a candle, and sink into a big bubble bath where I could soak away the ache in my shoulders from far too long behind the steering wheel.

That would definitely be the better choice.

But it wouldn't be the choice that would allow me to see Ethan, even for a few minutes.

So, when I pulled up to the four-way stop, instead of turning right, toward my shop and apartment, I took a left and headed to the community hall.

The parking lot was half full when I pulled in. The meeting had been going on a while, but with any luck, things would be winding down soon.

I snuck inside as quietly as possible, pulling my scarf off as I attempted to blend in near the back.

I found a spot along the far wall and had started to scan the room, looking for Ethan when the woman standing next to me nudged me in the ribs and handed me a copy of the agenda.

"We're almost done," she whispered. "Just talking about new permit applications." She jabbed a finger toward the bottom of the paper.

"Thanks." I smiled at her and continued to scan the full room in search of Ethan. I was glad the meeting was almost over. It wouldn't be long before I could get a hug and a kiss and head home to my warm, cozy bed.

I spotted Lauren and Brody sitting side by side on the far right. They had their heads tilted together, discussing something in hushed whispers. I shook my head with a smile as the councilwoman at the front of the room said something that caught my attention.

"A patio space in the plaza would offer guests and townspeople another option for a gathering space."

A *patio*? I nodded in agreement. If the Bean Bag put in some outdoor seating, that *would* be a welcome addition to the end of the plaza. Sitting in the warm sun, enjoying a fresh cinnamon bun and a cup of coffee would go right to the top of my weekday morning to-do list.

"The council is in agreement that any way we can attract more foot traffic to the plaza and encourage those people to stay longer will be mutually beneficial to all businesses."

I nodded along, but froze when I heard what she said next.

"As long as the proper liquor licensing was obtained, the council is in full support."

Liquor licensing?

The Bean Bag didn't serve alcohol.

Maybe they were talking about the old diner that Willa had run for longer than anyone could remember. But she hadn't changed anything—including the decor or the menu —for over forty years. It didn't seem feasible that she would put in patio seating.

I was exhausted and clearly my brain wasn't keeping up with what was happening, because there was no way that I heard correctly a moment later, when the councilwoman said, "Congratulations, Mr. Lyons. This council member looks forward to enjoying a cold beer on Peaks & Brews new patio this summer."

Peaks & Brews?

My stomach dropped.

As in, *Ethan's* brewery?

As in, the brewery that was only steps away from my quiet little bookshop?

I turned to the woman standing next to me. "What is she talking about?"

The woman handed me another piece of paper. The official proposal for an outdoor sitting space had been presented.

Small tables, tasteful lighting, seasonal planters.

The entire proposal had been crafted smoothly. It was polished. Planned.

"They just voted," the woman said. "Right before you walked in."

My mouth dropped open.

"It's going to be great, right?" The woman continued. "It's about time we had a patio in the plaza. It'll be a real draw. And on a nice warm summer night…"

I stopped listening. My ears buzzed and my vision blurred.

Surely, I misheard. There was no way that Ethan would put this together without talking to me about it.

After all, I was his neighbor. Our doors were only feet away from each other. We already had issues with noise when it came to book club nights. And a patio? With people drinking? Right outside my front door?

And he never even mentioned it.

We were together just over twenty-four hours ago. *Together*, together.

He could have asked me about it. Discussed what a patio would mean for Plot Twist. But he hadn't said a word.

Was that intentional?

Ethan knew I wasn't going to be at the meeting…*was that by design?*

So I couldn't protest?

My mind spun.

This couldn't be happening.

The meeting was adjourned. A whoop of joy caught my attention and I spun, seeing Ethan for the first time, high-fiving Brody in celebration.

I watched while he turned to accept a congratulatory handshake from someone I didn't recognize. He was smiling and laughing as though he hadn't just upended my entire world.

Like this wasn't something that would without a doubt impact *my* store, *my* business, *my* entire livelihood that I'd worked so hard to rebuild after so many years.

Yet, he'd never brought it up. Not once. Not while we were in my shop decorating, or lying in bed together, or sitting at his kitchen table pretending that we might be able to be something together. Might be able to be a *family*.

His eyes met mine then. A second later, his smile faltered.

I didn't wave. I couldn't move. I was frozen in place while my whole world shattered around me.

I was such a fool.

I'd been played.

I had to get out of there.

Ethan

Holy. Shit.

That was way easier than I would have guessed. I'd hardly been able to give the whole idea much thought yet, and just like that, with barely a question or a conversation, it was happening.

I chuckled a little under my breath and scrubbed a hand over my face while the reality of what I'd just signed up for sank in. One more thing to add to my already overflowing to-do list.

"Congrats, brother." Next to me, Brody held up his hand for a high five. "I look forward to having beers on the patio this summer."

"You and me both," I said. "And you'll earn those beers, too. I'm definitely going to need some help with this."

Before he could answer, we were joined by other business owners offering me congratulations and thanking me for bringing the idea of some outdoor seating to the plaza.

I shook hands with a council member and someone else clapped me on the back. "It's going to be a busy summer, Lyons."

I could only hope that the patio space would be as popular as everyone around me seemed to think it would be. Opening a new business was never easy, and Peaks & Brews was no exception. With the amount of overhead that had been required to get set up, turning much of a profit in our first year was going to be tricky. But outdoor seating had the potential to improve that bottom line.

It was everything I hoped for since the first time I looked at the old Chinese food restaurant and visualized what a brewery space could be and that I could be the one to turn it into something.

A huge smile on my face, I turned toward the crowd, scanning the room, and that's when I saw her.

Delaney.

She stood alone by the back wall, with her coat still on.

She'd made it after all.

My stomach flipped the way it always did when I saw her pretty face.

For half a second, I didn't register it. Just smiled like an idiot and lifted my hand in a half wave.

Then I saw the expression on her face.

No smile. None of her usual warmth. Just…flat.

Like she was holding back tears or something worse.

Before I could make a move toward her, she turned and slipped out the door. Fast.

Like a *get me the hell out of here* fast.

Shit.

Vaguely, I excused myself to whoever was listening, not waiting or caring whether anyone responded, as I hurried through the crowd after her.

By the time I made it outside, she was almost at her car on the other end of the parking lot.

"Delaney!" I called out. "Wait."

She stiffened, hesitating for a second before continuing her charge across the snowy parking lot to her car.

"Hey." I caught up, lightly grabbing her elbow. "What's going on? Where are you—"

She spun to face me. The hard look in her eyes stopped me as she thrust a package at me.

"Your labels." Her voice was ice cold. "But I don't suppose you really needed them at all, did you? It was just a way to keep me out of town a little longer."

"What?" I shook my head and tucked the package under my arm. "What's going on? What's wrong?"

"You're really asking me that right now?"

I blinked, feeling like I'd missed something critical. "I am...I... Delaney. What's going on? Did something happen in the city?"

"The city?" Her mouth dropped open in disbelief. "If we were in the city, instead of this small town where you and your family know everyone, I might have at least had a chance."

"A chance at what?" My head spun. I could not keep up. "I have no idea what you're talking about."

"A chance at not having my entire livelihood destroyed, Ethan. That's what." She jerked out of my touch and wrapped her arms around herself like a hug.

Yes. I definitely missed something critical. "What are you talking about?"

"You know that patio that just got cheers and high-fives?

The one that's going to go *right* in front of my store and be filled with rowdy people drinking alcohol and completely destroying the peaceful vibes of my bookstore? *That's* what I'm talking about."

"Wait." I opened my mouth and shut it again. "That's it? *That's* why you're upset?"

She took a step back as if I'd slapped her, and I instantly regretted my choice of words.

"I...it's..." My gut twisted to see the way she was looking at me. "It's nothing major, Delaney. It's just a few tables. Maybe some umbrellas and—"

"It's right there, Ethan," she cut me off. "Right out front of my door. The music. The loud patrons. Right outside my windows and the reading nook where *my* customers sit and read. Where kids come for story time. Where people gather to talk about books and things that resonate with something deep inside them. And now, right outside there's going to be a *bar.*" She blinked hard. "So, *yes*, Ethan. It really is something major. And you didn't even think to mention it to me."

I didn't mention it? But I must have. I searched my memory for the last few days and the time I'd spent with Delaney. Amazing time. All of it. We'd talked about so many things. And then we weren't talking at all. But...

Shit.

It had popped in my head at breakfast the day before, but then...

"Don't tell me it slipped your mind."

I swallowed down the words and tried again. "It didn't seem like that big a deal." The words sounded weak coming out of my mouth.

Her expression cracked. Even in the dimly lit parking lot, I could see the glisten of a tear in her eye before she swiped at her face with a mittened hand. "You made me feel like we were building something together, Ethan. Something real."

"We are."

"No." She shook her head. "*We* aren't. You were building something for *yourself.* And I was just…it doesn't matter."

"It does." I reached for her, but she stepped out of my reach. "That's not fair, Delaney."

"No?" she asked, her eyes shining now. "Then why didn't you say anything? Why didn't you tell me about what you were planning or ask me what I thought? Why didn't you talk to me about how it might impact *me*? Or my business. Or everything that *I've* built."

I didn't have a good answer.

I forgot. I didn't think of it. I didn't want to bother her when she was already so busy. It didn't seem important.

They all sounded like exactly what they were. Excuses.

"I should have told you," I said.

She pulled her coat tighter. "It's not even that you didn't tell me, Ethan. It's that you didn't even *consider* me."

"Delaney—"

"I'm such an idiot." Her voice cracked, but she didn't back down. "You waltzed in next door with all your charm, smooth talking, and flirty smiles. And like a love-sick fool, I fell for it."

My chest squeezed. "No. It's not—"

"I knew better," she continued with a scoff. "But I still let it happen. I let you make me feel like I mattered."

"You do!"

"Like this thing between us might actually be something real, and it might actually mean something."

"It *does*."

"Does it?" she snapped. "Because from where I'm standing, it looks like it was all smoke and mirrors while you buttered me up and made it nice and easy for you to push your own agenda."

She stepped back and looked away as if she couldn't stand to be so close to me.

"No." I shook my head. This was all wrong. "It wasn't—"

"You know what the worst part is?" she said quietly. "I let myself believe that you were different. That you weren't going to destroy me."

"Delaney. Please—"

"Good night, Ethan." She turned and closed the distance to her car.

I followed behind her because I couldn't seem to stop myself.

She didn't yell or slam the door. Worse, she got in and started the engine as if it were just another quiet ending to an evening.

Only it wasn't.

I took a step back to avoid being hit as she pulled out, her headlights sweeping across the lot that had started to fill with others leaving the meeting. I stood on the edge of the pavement and took two steps after her car as she turned onto the street, as if I could stop her, knowing there wasn't a damn thing I could do about it.

Instead, I stood there like a complete idiot who'd realized just a little too late that I'd gotten everything I wanted. And in the process, lost everything I needed.

Chapter Nineteen

Delaney

"You know, you're my first Christmas arrangement?" Charli, the owner of Alpenglow, smiled at me as she artfully arranged a pine bough with a sprig of holly in the oversized galvanized bucket outside my shop. "You're pretty smart for getting your order in early. I'll be busier than I can handle in a few weeks."

I smiled and rubbed my gloved hands together. "It has nothing to do with being smart," I told her. "I just happen to love Christmas and start my decorating earlier than most *normal* people. In fact, I think I showed great constraint waiting as long as I did."

"Your shop looks great," Charli said. "I don't know how it's going to go with a tree this year now that Poppy has started to get into everything." She chuckled. "It should be interesting."

Charli and her husband, Symon, were the proud parents of the cutest little girl I'd ever seen. Best friends who turned into more, theirs was one of the sweetest love stories in town.

Not that I had any interest in love stories of any kind at the moment.

"I'm sure it's going to be a great holiday," I said with as much enthusiasm as I could. If she noticed my mood, she was kind enough not to point it out. A small mercy I was grateful for.

The last few days since I'd discovered what Ethan had been up to behind my back had been awful. It was a physical pain in my chest to know that after all this time, and after coming so far, I'd fallen for a smooth talker who broke my heart once again.

It almost felt worse this time than it had with my ex. Maybe because with Ken, the signs had been there almost from the beginning, and I'd always sort of known how it was going to end. But with Ethan, I really and truly thought he was different. Worse, I'd let myself believe what we had was real.

I'd believed it with all my heart.

And now…

"Delaney?"

I shook my head, pulling myself from my thoughts when Charli waved a sprig of holly in my direction. "Sorry. I just…"

"You looked like you were about to cry," Charli said kindly. "Is everything okay?"

"It's fine," I lied. "I think maybe I'm just hungry." It was a terrible lie, and we both knew it. "Maybe I should leave you to it and go grab something from the Bean Bag for lunch. Do you want anything?"

"I'm good, thanks. But don't let me stop you."

I was halfway across the plaza to the coffee shop when I saw them.

Quinn and Ethan, walking hand in hand, headed straight toward me.

It was too late to turn around. There was nowhere to go.

"Bookstore lady!"

Too late.

I did my best to paste a smile on my face as Quinn released her dad's hand and sprinted toward me. "Hey, kiddo." She wrapped her arms around me in a spontaneous hug that almost cracked me. I swallowed hard to keep from crying. "Shouldn't you be at school?"

Quinn pulled back. "Dentist appointment." She shrugged. "Not enough time to go back before the end of the day."

"Makes sense." I nodded before reluctantly looking up at Ethan, who'd joined us.

"Hey," he said as if it were any other day and he hadn't just completely shattered my heart.

"Hi." My voice was thinner than I meant it to be.

The silence stretched out between us way longer than it should have.

Quinn looked between us, her brows knitting together in question.

"Did you get your inventory shipment okay?" Ethan asked.

"Yup." I nodded. "It's kept me pretty busy the last few days, stocking all the new products."

"I bet." He looked like he was going to say something more, but pressed his lips together tightly instead.

"The labels work out okay?"

I couldn't meet his gaze for more than a few seconds at a time. Not without remembering the way he'd looked in the community hall, celebrating his victory that had completely blindsided me.

"They did," he said. "Thanks again for picking them up."

We stood silently in the middle of the plaza. The cold air did nothing to chill the anger, confusion, and stupid ache in my chest that pulsed with heat.

Quinn's gaze flicked from me to her dad. "Okay...weird energy here." She waved a mittened hand between us. "What's—"

"I should get back inside," I said quickly. "Thanks for saying hi, Quinn."

"Can I come by later and check out your new books?"

I hesitated, but only for a second. "Of course." I aimed a small smile in her direction.

"Maybe we can—"

"Right." I cut Ethan off before he could finish his thought. "I should get back."

I turned and walked back to the store, forgetting entirely that I'd planned to grab some food. I blinked hard and did my best to ignore the burning at the corner of my eyes while I pretended that every step I took didn't feel like I was leaving everything important behind me.

Ethan

Quinn was quiet for maybe ten steps after Delaney walked away.

Truthfully, that was about nine more than I'd expected.

"What was that?"

I glanced over at her. "What was what?"

Her eyes widened. "That." She pointed toward Plot Twist, where Delaney had just slipped inside. "You and

Delaney," Quinn continued, skipping the use of her nick-name. "You guys are being all weird. And you didn't even try the gross stuff."

I'd wanted to pull Delaney into my arms and kiss her more than I wanted to take my next breath, but that was no longer an option. My heart ached with the loss.

"She looked like she was about to cry, and you...well, you looked like a bit of a jerk."

"A jerk?"

She nodded but didn't back down. "So, what's going on?"

I shoved my hands deep into my pockets. "It's nothing."

"Nothing? It sure didn't *feel* like nothing."

I exhaled through my nose and started to move. "We're fine."

"Now you're lying."

"Quinn," I said a little sharper than I intended. "It's adult stuff." I softened my voice. "Don't worry about it."

She stopped walking. "Wow."

With a sigh, I turned to face her.

She crossed her arms and glared at me. "Since when do you pull that card?"

I hesitated. "I didn't mean it like that."

"Yes, you did. That's why you said it." Her jaw clenched the way it always did when she was trying not to cry. Only, it wasn't usually me who was making her upset.

"I'm sorry," I said genuinely. "It's just..." I glanced to my right. "Let's stop by the Sugar Shack and grab some chocolates for family dinner."

Quinn narrowed her eyes as if she were trying to decide between trying to push for more or the lure of chocolate. "We don't usually take chocolates."

"I thought it might be a nice treat."

"Is Delaney coming to family dinner?"

I froze mid-step and exhaled in a huff. "Drop it, Quinn."

"So there's something to drop?" Before I could respond, she continued. "You're just trying to distract me with chocolate."

"I'm not."

"You are." Her voice rose. "You don't want to talk about what's really going on with you, so you're going to buy me off with chocolates and pretend everything's fine when it's—"

"Enough!"

The word hit the air like a sharp slap.

Quinn took a step back and stared at me. Her bottom lip quivered.

We didn't do this.

We didn't snap. We didn't raise our voices. And we definitely didn't shut down.

But now, here we were.

And for so many reasons, I hated it.

She turned away without another word and started to walk ahead of me, arms crossed and chin tucked down.

I stood there for a second and watched her go.

And for the second time in less than a week, I found myself frozen in place, realizing a little too late that I'd made the wrong call.

Chapter Twenty

Ethan

The table was set, the food was hot, and the energy was off.

Really off.

Normally, family dinners were loud and chaotic in the very best way, with too many voices all talking over one another. Grayson giving Preston crap about something, probably about forgetting the napkins or buns or some other equally basic item he'd been assigned but still managed to forget. Brody pretending he was the head of the family because he was the oldest, and the rest of us letting him think it.

But tonight?

Everyone was polite.

Too polite.

Quinn sat next to Reid, next to the empty seat across from me.

Delaney's seat.

I tried not to look at it, or acknowledge that her absence was the reason everyone was acting so weird.

"This is good." Preston handed the platter of roast beef to Avery. "Better than usual."

Brody frowned, but resisted the urge to fire back some sort of comment about how the only thing Preston could cook was breakfast cereal.

"No, it's not," Quinn blurted, and I shot her a look. "Sorry, Uncle Brody," she added quickly. "But roast beef isn't my favorite."

"I know." Brody nodded graciously. "It's okay. I was going to make burgers, but I wanted to…"

He let the thought trail away, and I swallowed hard, picking at my mashed potatoes. He'd wanted to make something *special* because Delaney was supposed to be there and it would have been her first Lyonses' family dinner. But I had to go fuck it all up.

"More gravy?"

"No one wants more gravy, Dad!" Quinn dropped her fork on her plate with a loud clatter.

"Quinn." I shot her a warning glance.

She gritted her teeth and picked up her water glass.

Things had only gone from bad to worse between us since we'd run into Delaney in the plaza the day before, but I did not need it coming to a head at the dinner table in front of everyone.

Thankfully, she went back to picking at her dinner, but as soon as I thought I was in the clear, Avery set down her wine glass and said, "Where's Delaney tonight, Ethan?"

I flinched and set my fork down slowly. "She had things to do at the shop."

I didn't miss the way Quinn looked up and glared at me. Neither did Reid, by the way his eyebrows shot up.

"That's weird," Avery continued. "She said she was really looking forward to coming."

"She changed her mind."

That did it.

Once more, Quinn dropped her fork onto her plate. The clatter bounced off every wall in the room.

"No, she didn't," Quinn announced. "She didn't change her mind," she snapped. "You hurt her, Dad."

"Quinn." My voice held a warning.

Everyone at the table went still. All eyes turned to me.

Brody cleared his throat. "Kiddo, I—"

"You didn't see her," Quinn went on, ignoring her uncle. "She was trying not to cry and Dad won't even talk about it. He told me it was nothing and not to worry about it. But I *am* worrying about it."

"Quinn," I tried again. "That's enough."

"It's not!" She shoved her chair back. It fell with a bang on the hardwood, but she didn't care. "I *like* her, Dad." Tears streamed down my daughter's face. "I told you not to be gross." Her voice cracked. "I didn't say you had to screw everything up."

And then she was gone.

I flinched as the sound of the bathroom door slamming down the hall resounded through the silent house.

For a moment, everyone was still. Avery stood a beat later, dropped her napkin on her plate of untouched food and, with a disapproving glance in my direction, followed her out of the room.

The rest of us sat in heavy silence.

Grayson was the first to speak. "So," he said slowly. "Are you going to tell us what the hell happened?"

I ran a hand down my face and took a breath. "It's not a big deal."

"Doesn't look that way from where I'm sitting," Preston said.

Reid crossed his arms and stared me down. "It's clearly a big deal to Quinn."

My eldest brother pushed his plate out of the way and leaned forward, elbows on the table. His voice was calm but firm. "Ethan. What did you do?"

I exhaled, already exhausted, but there didn't seem to be any way out of discussing this with my brothers. "Honestly, I don't know." Before they could object, I continued. "She showed up to the community meeting, but she got there late. Right after the vote on the patio. I didn't even notice she was there until afterward, and when I saw her...well, she was upset."

"Upset?"

I nodded. "I caught up with her in the parking lot and she laid into me because I didn't tell her about the whole thing."

"You didn't tell her?" Reid asked. "Seriously?"

"So Delaney found out you were putting a patio out front of both your stores *after* the vote passed?"

I had to admit, it sounded even shittier when Grayson laid it out like that.

"Why the fuck wouldn't you talk to her about something that major?" Brody shook his head incredulously.

"I don't know women," Preston chimed in. "But, *damn*, brother."

"What?" I raised my hands. "I didn't even think about it, and I certainly didn't think it would be a problem." I hated how defensive I sounded. "It's only a few tables. It's not really even in front of her space. It's just..."

"You're missing the point," Reid said.

Grayson nodded in agreement with his twin. "Completely."

"She's not mad about the tables," Brody added. "Well, she might be. But I don't think that's the problem here."

"Then what?"

I truly wanted to know, because every time I thought maybe I was getting close to understanding how I'd managed to screw things up so badly, it still didn't make any sense.

My brothers all exchanged glances, but it was Brody who said, "She's upset because she thought she mattered to you."

"But she—"

"She supported you." Brody cut me off smoothly. "She made room for you *and* Quinn in her life. She was in it with you, man. And then, at your very first opportunity, you went and showed her exactly how much she *doesn't* matter to you."

That landed.

Hard.

Right in the center of my chest.

"And then she finds out from a room full of strangers and townspeople that you made a decision that will directly affect her and her business." Preston shook his head. "Come on, man."

"I agree that the patio itself isn't that big of a deal," Grayson added before I could recover. "Just a few tables, and I know the plan you have is simple and unobtrusive. It probably won't impact her business at all."

"But Delaney doesn't know that," Reid continued. "Because you didn't give her that chance to understand. You didn't even consider her in this."

"We warned you, Ethan," Brody said with a look of disappointment only a big brother could pull off. "When we were talking the other night. We more or less *told* you that Delaney would care."

"You screwed up," Reid confirmed with a nod. "Big time."

Shit.

They weren't wrong.

"Hell," Preston said. "She probably would have helped you design the whole thing. But you didn't *ask*."

And suddenly, it was so obvious.

I was a first-class asshole.

Worse. I was an oblivious asshole.

It wasn't so much about zoning or sidewalk space or being in front of Plot Twist. It was the fact that I'd made a choice that directly impacted her world, and I didn't even stop to consider her or take the time to loop her in.

"Honestly, it wasn't about blindsiding her."

"We believe you," Reid said. "But does she?"

She didn't. I shook my head. She'd said as much.

I'd charmed my way into her life, made her feel safe, *loved*. And then I went and proved that I was just another man putting himself first.

Fuck.

"I didn't even think…"

"About her," Reid finished for me. "And that's the problem."

"Brother." Brody shook his head. "You've spent too long only thinking about you and Quinn. Even when you were married, you didn't have to consider Polly because she did enough of that for herself. But it's not just the two of you anymore."

"Not if you want this thing with Delaney to work."

I did.

I very much did.

I stared at my plate and then at the seat where Delaney should have been.

And for the first time, it all became very, *very* clear.

Delaney wasn't upset because of the patio.

She was hurt because I didn't make space for *us*.

I hadn't just let her down. I'd made her believe she didn't matter. And fixing that? It was going to take more than charm and apologies. It was going to take more than words. It had to mean something.

And I'd make damn sure it did.

My gaze traveled toward the hallway where Quinn had disappeared.

Delaney wasn't the only one I needed to make things right with.

I'd fix it.

All of it.

Delaney

By the time the group got around to discussing the grand gesture, I was completely over it. When I told Rochelle she could have the night off, and I would lead the book club discussion because I wouldn't be attending the Lyonses' family dinner after all, I'd completely forgotten that it was the romance meeting.

"And what do you think about the way the hero groveled in chapter fifteen?"

A few scattered murmurs filled the cozy corner of the store. Half a bottle of wine sat on the table, with a few cookie crumbs left on the platter.

I blinked at the group of familiar faces that were all staring at me, waiting for my opinion.

Right. Book club.

Focus, Delaney.

"I mean, I thought maybe he could have…"

"Done *something*," Joanne jumped in. "I mean, groveling is fine and all."

"But back it up with *action*." Nora nodded along.

They weren't wrong. An apology was one thing. But for the hero to do something to show the heroine how he'd changed…that was the real win.

My mind flashed to Ethan, but I immediately pushed it away. Life wasn't a romance novel, and Ethan wasn't the hero of my story.

That much was clear.

No matter how much I wanted it to be true.

"That's a great point," I added, happy to contribute something considering I'd spent most of the meeting lost in thought about the dinner I should have been at. "When trust is broken in real life, it takes more than groveling to make it better."

The conversation picked up again without me, and I let it. I made a mental note to let Rochelle take over at the next romance book club meeting. Usually, it was one of my favorite clubs to facilitate, but I didn't usually have a broken heart of my own.

I nodded along as someone else brought up tropes, but my mind drifted away again. This time, to Ethan and the way he'd looked at me in the parking lot, like he truly didn't know why I was upset. And then again in the plaza, like he still didn't understand what had broken between us. Or why.

Maybe he didn't.

But how could he *not* get it?

After what felt like a torturously long time, I glanced at the clock over the mantel and clapped my hands together, forcing a smile onto my face. "Okay, group. We'll have to wrap it up here for the night. Next month, we're diving into holiday romances. Check your email for a list of recommended books." I put a smile I didn't feel on my face. "And prepare yourself for snowed-in cabins, hot chocolate, and flannel-clad heroes with all the Christmas carols."

"My favorite kind." Joanne wiggled her eyebrows.

I offered her a soft smile, because I didn't trust myself to speak without crying, and looked away.

Mercifully, most of the ladies trailed out of the shop without trying to engage me in further conversation. A small part of me hoped that I wasn't putting out unfriendly and unwelcoming vibes, but a larger part of me couldn't be bothered to care.

It was all I could do not to burst into tears of anger, as my emotions battled inside me. What I really needed was to lock the door and escape upstairs to my bed.

"That was a lovely discussion, dear."

I braced myself before I turned around and frantically scanned my brain for a way out of the discussion I knew was coming next.

"Tilley." I turned around with a very fake smile on my face to see our town busybody, bundled up in her winter coat with a massive hand-knit scarf wrapped around her neck. I'd managed to avoid eye contact with her for most of the evening, but now I was cornered.

Her eyes twinkled. I knew exactly what she wanted to talk about.

"I'm glad you enjoyed it, Tilley," I said. "I was just locking up."

"Oh, I won't keep you."

Yet, that's exactly what she was about to do. Normally, I didn't mind spending a few minutes talking to Tilley Beckett. After all, she was a sweet old lady, and besides the fact that anything you told her would spread like a wildfire in the wind within seconds, she was generally quite harmless.

"I thought your insights on the romance in the book were quite…insightful."

I tried not to groan.

"Almost as if you have some personal experience in the matter."

She blinked her lashes and winked at me.

Before I could deny it, or set her straight because the gossip mill clearly hadn't made its rounds yet about the most recent status of my relationship with Ethan, she opened her mouth again.

"Aren't the Lyons having their family dinner tonight?"

It never ceased to amaze me the information this woman had at her fingertips.

I shrugged.

"Shouldn't you be there, dear?"

No. I shouldn't. Family dinners were for *family*. And Ethan made it very clear by his actions that I wasn't considered that way. Not at all.

Not that I was about to tell Tilley any of that. "We're just neighbors, Tilley."

"Now, now." She cut me off. "Everyone knows you and that handsome brewmaster next door are the latest hot thing. The two of you have created quite a buzz around town."

I forced myself to keep my face expressionless.

"From what I hear, he's quite smitten with you."

The fact that news of our breakup hadn't traveled to Tilley yet surprised me, but it only meant that Ethan hadn't said anything to anyone, because I knew I hadn't. Not even to Lauren. It was too painful to admit that I'd gotten it wrong with Ethan.

I forced a humorless laugh. "I'm not sure what people think, Tilley. But whatever it is, they're wrong. Ethan and I—"

"Oh." She tilted her head and narrowed her eyes.

Shit.

I realized too late that I should have just kept my mouth shut.

Tilley tapped one finger against her lips. "I see…"

I shook my head, but didn't have a chance to tell her that she didn't *see* at all, because there was nothing to see.

"There's trouble brewing," she said after a moment. "Love can be tricky."

"It's not like—"

"Whatever's happened, I hope that Lyons boy is smart enough to know how to fix it."

I blinked at the old woman in disbelief. She reached out and squeezed my arm for a moment.

I wasn't sure what to say to that, and thankfully, Nora called to Tilley from the door, where she waited.

Tilley gave me one last look. "You, my dear, are the type of woman who deserves the grandest of grand gestures."

My heart clenched, and I blinked hard to keep the tears at bay as she turned and swept out of the store with the rest of the group, leaving me standing there, a little bit breathless and totally heartbroken.

Sure, Tilley was missing a few details, but there was a reason she had the reputation in Trickle Creek that she did. She was spot-on.

Except for one thing. I didn't need the grand gesture.

I only wanted to feel like I mattered.

And right now…I wasn't so sure I did.

Ethan

The plaza was quiet by the time I left Brody's place.

Quinn was so upset with me, she refused to talk to me. I could have pushed the issue and forced her to come home with me, but what was the point?

She was in good hands with my family, and Reid and Avery agreed to take her home with them and make sure she got to school the next morning. It seemed like the best option. Particularly considering I had a few things to work through on my own.

Quite a few.

But I still hated leaving her behind. We'd never been like this before. We'd never fought to the point where she refused to speak to me. And I couldn't blame her. My heart ached, knowing I'd let my baby girl down.

I told myself the quiet was good. A night alone would give me a chance to think through some things. But I wasn't ready to go back to my empty house yet, so I'd made the decision to detour to the brewery instead.

I hadn't planned to see her.

When I rounded the corner by Earth's Own, I stopped short and pressed up against the wall. A small group of women filtered out of Plot Twist in a burst of chatter and laughter.

Book club.

When I invited Delaney to family dinner, she said she was going to get Rochelle to lead it. But there she was, standing in the doorway, watching the women walk away.

I was pretty sure she couldn't see me, but I stayed back anyway. I wasn't ready to face her yet. Not when I was only just beginning to understand what exactly I'd broken.

I watched as she flipped the lock and walked back

toward the front counter. She placed her hand flat on the top, and the whole thing swayed under her touch.

A breath caught in my throat, but by some miracle, it didn't topple over. It was only a matter of time before the stupid thing collapsed altogether.

Inside the shop, the lights dimmed. Delaney left the counter, but instead of walking to the back of her shop and heading up to her apartment, she moved back to the front window.

She didn't see me, and I felt like maybe I was intruding on a private moment when I saw her press her palm lightly against the glass. It was only for a brief moment.

But I'd seen it.

Hell, I felt it in my gut.

She was sad. She was hurt.

This thing between us wasn't casual or *small* at all. It was real, and it was worth so much more than I'd been giving it.

But that changed now.

My brothers were right. Delaney wasn't upset about the patio—although I could have been a hell of a lot more thoughtful about that, too.

It was about so much more, and it had taken me way too long to figure that out. I just hoped like hell that it wasn't too late.

Delaney

The shop was finally quiet.

Normally, hosting book club energized me. But it had been a long day. A long week.

I should have immediately gone up to bed, but something pulled me back to the window and the deserted plaza outside. Most of the shops had small apartments above them, but usually the evenings were quiet.

With a sigh, I realized how much that would change with a patio right outside my door.

I blew out a breath, but the flash of anger I might have expected never came. It was hard to be angry when I was so damn sad at everything I'd lost.

I pressed a hand to the window and just for a moment allowed myself to hope that Ethan was outside and that he'd be walking across the plaza to my shop. That he would knock on my door and…say something. Fix this thing that was broken.

But there was nothing but emptiness outside. A moment was all I could afford to allow myself.

I stepped away from the window and turned to survey the shop.

My shop.

My dream I'd built from the ground up. I'd scrimped and saved and sacrificed for Plot Twist. No, it wasn't perfect, and all the couches and chairs might be second-hand, the pillows collected from thrift stores. The shelves full of inventory that I'd personally sourced and selected. The tables with indie authors I'd read and recommended myself.

Every day was hard. Balancing the books that sometimes didn't want to add up no matter what I did wasn't easy, but it was *mine*.

I'd already lost a dream to a man who made promises he couldn't keep and, when I wasn't looking, made all the important decisions without me.

I wouldn't do it again.

I couldn't.

No matter how much my heart longed for him.

Chapter Twenty-One

Delaney

I knew better than to make them wait.

It had only been two days since the romance book club met and already the women were blowing up my inbox with inquiries about the list of holiday books I'd promised them.

Out of all our book clubs, the romance club was definitely full of the most avid readers. Those ladies could put down three or four books a week. Which was why they were the only club I gave a list to, instead of only one book to discuss.

Normally, I had the selections chosen right away, but I couldn't seem to bring myself to even go near the romance shelves, let alone pull out the best holiday books I could find. Maybe I was being dramatic, but the last thing on my mind was love.

Yes, I was definitely being dramatic. But I didn't care. I was allowed to wallow in my own self-pity. At least for a little bit longer.

"Rochelle." I finally gave in and handed my employee the clipboard where I'd written a few titles before scratching them out. "Can you please pull together some holiday romances for book club. I just—"

The bells over the door saved me from an explanation, not that one was needed. I didn't generally talk about my personal life with my staff, but Rochelle wasn't stupid. She'd noticed a change in me, and probably the very noticeable absence of the brewmaster from next door, who, up until recently, had popped in at least once a day.

"I got this." She gave me a soft smile, and I nodded gratefully before I turned to greet the new customer.

My heart caught in my throat. "Quinn."

She raised a mittened hand. "Hey, bookstore lady."

"Hey, yourself."

I hadn't seen her since the other day in the plaza when I'd run into her and Ethan. It had been awkward and awful. Besides, she was way too smart not to have figured out that something was wrong. Which probably explained her absence from the store. I couldn't help but wonder what Ethan had told her.

"You haven't been around for a while."

She shifted her weight from foot to foot, like she wasn't sure what to say.

"I've missed you."

Her head shot up. "You have?"

"Of course." I took a few steps toward her, afraid she might turn around and bolt. She seemed so uncertain and not at all like the Quinn I'd gotten to know.

"I almost didn't come."

"You know you're always welcome here," I said softly. "No matter what's…" I couldn't finish the thought, but she did it for me.

"What's going on with you and my dad?"

I nodded, and she shrugged.

"I'm mad at him," she blurted after a moment. "Like, *really* mad."

That hurt my heart in a way I hadn't expected.

"Oh, Quinn." I reached for her and led her to the oversized chair she preferred. She sank into the soft cushions immediately, and I perched across from her on the ottoman. "You don't need to be mad at him."

"Yes," she said softly but firmly. "I do." She took a deep breath. "You don't understand. Dad and I...we tell each other everything. We always have. But now...this thing with you guys." She waved her hand around. "Well, it doesn't feel good. And it doesn't feel good the way he won't talk to me about it."

I nodded because it was the only thing I *could* do. She was right. None of this felt good.

"I thought maybe if I stayed away from here, he might tell me...well, it doesn't matter. It's stupid."

"It's not stupid," I said quickly. "None of this is stupid. I'll be honest, I don't know what the right answer is either."

"You don't?"

I shook my head. "But I do know what the wrong thing is."

She looked at me, waiting for the information that would make it all better. Unfortunately, I didn't have it. But I hoped what I *did* have to say might ease things a little. "Being mad at your dad isn't going to help things," I said gently. "I know it might feel like it will, but it won't. And the other important thing is that you don't have to pick sides. That's not fair to you. None of this is your fault."

She swallowed hard and nodded, ducking her head.

"So you and me," she said after a moment. "We can still be friends?"

My throat burned, and I blinked hard, determined not to cry in front of her.

"We better still be friends," I said with a smile. "Because we never stopped."

She smiled then, even if it was a little sad.

I squeezed her hand and just held it for a moment before clearing my throat sharply. "Now, are you ready for a new book? Because I just got my last inventory shipment in and I've been holding a few behind the counter for you."

Her eyes lit up, and just like that, the air between us cleared.

"Some more of that fantasy?" she asked hopefully. "Nothing with the gross stuff this time."

I laughed. The last book I'd given her only had a kiss between the two leads, but obviously even that much romance was too much right now.

I couldn't disagree with her.

"Strong female lead, epic world building, and absolutely no gross stuff," I said. "You know I'd never steer you wrong."

She followed me to the front counter, where I retrieved the books I'd been saving for her.

"So cool." She ran her hand over the cover of the first book and then spontaneously wrapped her arms around me in a tight hug. "Thank you, Delaney."

My heart caught in my throat, and I squeezed her tightly in return.

It didn't fix everything.

But it was something.

And for the moment, that was going to have to be enough.

Ethan

The lasagna was still bubbling when I pulled it from the oven. The smell of it made my mouth water in anticipation, and just as I hoped it would, it also drew Quinn from her room and into the kitchen.

"Smells good," she said begrudgingly.

It wasn't much. But at least she was talking to me now.

The lasagna had taken me all afternoon to put together. But it was Quinn's favorite, and well worth the effort if it meant my daughter would at least give me the opportunity to explain…and apologize.

I set the pan on the table along with a Caesar salad and a basket of garlic bread.

Quinn raised an eyebrow in question as I sat down across from her. "What's the occasion?"

"No occasion." I shrugged. "I thought it would be nice to have a home-cooked meal."

"Lasagna is my favorite."

I shrugged again and offered her a wry grin. "Is it?"

"You know it is." She finally cracked and gave me a small smile in return. "Even if it is an obvious peace offering, I'll take it."

I reached forward and grabbed the serving spatula to offer her the corner piece, just the way she liked, before dishing up my own.

A few quiet bites passed between us before I dared to broach the subject I'd been avoiding. "I'm sorry."

She paused, a forkful of lasagna halfway to her lips.

"For how I handled everything," I elaborated. "I shouldn't have treated you like a little kid, Quinn. I know you're not. It's just sometimes…" I set my knife and fork down and sat back in my chair. "It's hard for me to remember that you're getting really grown-up and you can…"

"Handle the truth," she finished for me.

"Yeah." I nodded. "And I never should have snapped at you and shut you down the way I did. I'm sorry."

Her face softened a little. "You were upset."

"That's not an excuse," I said quickly.

She hesitated for a moment before setting her fork down. "You kind of scared me a little when you got mad."

That gutted me.

"I hate that," I said quietly. "I want you to always feel like you can talk to me, Quinn. Even when I make a mess of things. Maybe *especially* when I mess things up. I am really sorry, kiddo."

After a moment, she looked up and gave me a small smile. "It's okay." She ripped a piece of bread off and stuffed it in her mouth.

It wasn't. But it would be.

We both resumed eating in a newly peaceful silence. After a few minutes, Quinn said, "I saw Delaney today."

I froze for a moment before putting the forkful of salad in my mouth and chewing thoughtfully. "Oh yeah?"

"Yup." Quinn reached for more garlic toast. "She told me not to be so hard on you."

A smile twitched at my lips. "She did, did she?"

"Yup. She also said that we were still going to be friends no matter what."

My stomach twisted. "Of course you are."

"What about you guys?"

Quinn asked the question so frankly, it took me off guard.

"Are you still going to be friends?"

More than anything, I wanted to be friends with Delaney.

No. Not true.

I wanted to be more than friends.

I took a deep breath and told Quinn the truth. "I hope so." I kept my tone even. "In fact, I've been thinking a lot about that lately and about how badly I handled everything with her."

Quinn nodded sagely as if she, too, had spent some time thinking exactly that.

"The truth is, I was so focused on the way things always had been, that I didn't stop to consider what they were growing and changing to be. And what they *could* be. I didn't stop to consider how my choices and decisions might affect Delaney, and when you're in a relationship, that's exactly what you should do. Does that make sense?"

"I think so." She chewed thoughtfully before adding, "You hurt her."

The words were so simple. But so accurate. And they hit right in the heart.

"I did." I swallowed hard. "But I didn't mean to."

"I know you didn't, Dad." Quinn lifted her fork in the air and stared at me for a moment. "But does she?"

"Honestly, I'm not sure," I said, opting for the truth. "But I hope she will."

She tilted her head, and for the first time, I could see the wisdom in my little girl and how grown-up she'd become. Especially when she said, "Then you're going to have to show her that, Dad."

"You're exactly right, kiddo. Exactly right."

She shrugged and popped another bite of lasagna in her mouth. "I know."

I couldn't help but laugh.

We ate the rest of our dinner with easy conversation about Quinn's school and her classmates. It felt normal again. Or at least, like it would be soon.

Later, after the dishes were cleared and homework was done, I knocked on Quinn's bedroom door.

"Come in."

She was in bed under a pile of blankets, the glow of her bedside lamp giving her enough light to read by.

I hadn't tucked her in for years, but I hovered in the doorway like I used to when she was young.

She set the paperback down when I walked in. "What's up?"

I hesitated for a moment. "I just wanted to say good night and..." I gestured with my head toward her bed. "Can I sit?"

She didn't answer, but scooted over and patted the bed next to her. I reached out and smoothed a piece of hair off her forehead. She didn't pull away.

"I just want you to know that I am going to try to fix things with Delaney," I said softly.

She blinked up at me. "How?"

I blew out a breath. "I'll start with an apology, but I know it needs to be more."

She nodded, but didn't speak.

"I'm going to show her that she matters," I continued. "*Really* matters."

"Good."

I smiled a little. "I know I screwed up, kiddo. But if she'll let me, I am going to fix it."

"You better," Quinn murmured. "Because I like her. A lot."

"So do I," I said softly.

"So?" Quinn straightened up in bed. "Do you have a plan yet?"

"As a matter of fact," I told her, "I do."

Her eyes lit up.

"And I'm going to need your help."

"Obviously." She rolled her eyes before a yawn took over.

"We'll talk about it tomorrow," I said. "I still have a few details I need to discuss with your Uncle Reid first."

To my surprise, she accepted that and held her arms out for a hug.

I kissed her forehead. "Love you, kiddo."

"Love you too, Dad."

I stood and was halfway to the door when she called out again. "Hey, Dad?"

I turned. "Yeah?"

"She looked like she missed you."

The lump in my throat was instant.

"I miss her, too."

Chapter Twenty-Two

Delaney

That morning, I'd come up with a dozen different ways to get out of it.

And then promptly rejected them all.

Besides, getting out of the shop and my tiny apartment would do me good. I knew that.

I'd been avoiding...well, everyone and everything since Ethan and I blew up.

I knew I couldn't hide forever.

Still, it wasn't going to be easy to be at a town-wide fundraising event with every eye on me and Ethan. And it wouldn't just be Tilley Beckett sticking her nose into our business.

It would be everyone.

There was no way that the news of our breakup hadn't traveled all around town by now. I hadn't missed the whispers and knowing glances.

If there had been any way to get out of it, I would have.

"Delaney! There you are!" Tilley called out moments

after I stepped inside the community hall. She swept across the old wood floor in a flurry of shawls. She waved her clipboard in the air. "Perfect timing. I need one more set of hands sorting and tagging the new donations. Are you okay with that?"

I didn't have a chance to answer, not that it would have mattered. Tilley always had her own agenda; everyone just kind of went along with it, and somehow things always got done.

"Great!" She grabbed my arm, spinning me around. "Ethan, dear! I found you a partner. You're with Delaney."

I blinked. *What?*

In a town full of people, what were the odds I would get paired up in a fundraiser with Ethan Lyons? It was a rhetorical question, because the answer was currently smiling and fluttering her eyelashes at me expectantly.

"Is that okay, Delaney?"

"Of course." I put the most neutral expression on my face that I could manage. "Why wouldn't it be?"

"Great." Tilley took my elbow and led me over to where Ethan was surrounded by what looked like dozens of boxes of jackets and other items of clothing. "Ethan can fill you in on what needs to be done." She gave me a wink. "Have fun, you two."

"Hey," he said, his voice low. "I didn't know you'd volunteered for this, too."

I nodded. "Anything for the community, right?"

He smiled, but it didn't quite reach his eyes. "Right."

"So," I picked up a pair of socks, "what are we doing here?"

With the work as a buffer between everything we weren't saying to each other, Ethan took a few minutes to explain the simple task of sorting the socks and sweaters into different boxes by size and gender.

We settled into the work. All around us, the fundraiser buzzed with energy. People were laughing and chatting while children chased one another around the coat racks. And of course, Tilley was in the middle of it all with her clipboard, like she was planning a military operation.

I focused on the work.

Ethan set his box down next to mine. "These gloves are barely used. Maybe someone bought them and changed their mind."

"It happens." I lifted a scarf from the pile. "This one looks brand-new, too."

"Maybe the same person." Ethan shrugged.

I nodded.

We fell into an uneasy silence.

"I saw the book tree in the shop window," he said after a few minutes, quieter now. "It looks really cool."

"Thanks." I'd worked on the book tree over a few days and was really happy with how it'd turned out. "I've been wanting to do one for years," I said. "I just never had enough time to get all my decorating done *and* do the tree." I trailed off, because he and Quinn, and their extra help, was the reason I had enough time this year.

"Well, it looks great. Perfect for your shop."

I nodded and grabbed a coat. "The holiday season is coming fast."

Ethan chuckled a little. "Don't rush it. It's only the middle of November."

I shrugged and tried not to smile. It was too easy to fall into a natural rhythm with him. "After Halloween, it's all Christmas. All the time."

"I am releasing a winter lager next week, does that count?"

I gave him a soft smile. "It does."

Another silence. Longer this time.

He picked up a coat and cleared his throat. "Business is good?"

I nodded. "Steady, which is good. I think the book tree helps."

"I'm sure it does." He smiled and looked like he might say something more. "You're really good at that stuff. Inviting people in."

His eyes met mine, and for a second, it felt *normal* again. The way things used to be.

I hated how much I missed that easiness between us.

He shifted and took a step closer. "Delaney, look—"

"It's fine," I cut in quickly, forcing my attention back to the box. "We're neighbors. It doesn't have to be weird."

"It does feel weird, doesn't it?"

"It doesn't have to," I said too fast. "We're just volunteering here, Ethan. Let's just...let's just get this done."

He didn't speak for a beat and then finally nodded slowly. "Okay. Let's just do this."

I hated how distant I sounded. How cold and unfeeling I was being. The truth was, I had *too* many feelings. Working so close to him was torture. I just needed to get through it and get away before I forgot how he'd hurt me and I let myself feel anything more.

We sorted without talking for a few more minutes. The silence between us built until it was almost too much.

"The kids' jackets either look brand-new, like they were outgrown before they were worn, or they look a little too well-loved. There doesn't seem to be much in between."

"I can tell you from experience," Ethan said, "there is no

in-between when it comes to kids' clothes. Half the winter jackets I've bought for Quinn over the years were returned before she ever got to wear them."

I gave him a tight smile.

"I saw her the other day," I offered finally. "She came into the shop."

"She told me."

That surprised me, although I wasn't sure why. "I told her to come by whenever. I hope that's okay."

"Of course. Why wouldn't it be?"

There were so many things I wanted to say, but I needed to protect myself. The wound was still too raw. Instead, I nodded. "Okay, good."

There was nothing else I could say, not without breaking down.

I turned and gave all my attention to the remaining items in my box.

The sooner we finished our pile, the sooner I could escape.

He didn't push again or offer any more conversation.

We finished our job in silence.

And it had never felt louder.

Ethan

The second I stepped outside into the brisk November day, I could breathe, and it had nothing to do with the fresh air.

Working side by side with Delaney for the afternoon had been torture. All I wanted to do was pull her into my arms, tell her how sorry I was about...well, everything. But every time the words were about to come out of my mouth, I stopped myself.

Not because I didn't want to tell her those things. I did. More than anything.

But I needed to do it right. I'd already been a giant idiot.

I knew I was only going to get one shot at making it better. And I wasn't going to blow it by fumbling over my words in the middle of the Jacket Racket fundraiser, surrounded by the entire town.

I shoved my hands in my pockets and started to walk toward the plaza. I hadn't intended to go back to the brewery; my staff handled things just fine without me. But I needed to move. I needed to think.

Delaney's voice echoed in my head: "We're neighbors. It doesn't have to be weird."

Weird?

It wasn't just weird. It was awful.

And it wasn't just what she said. It was the way she'd said it. Her voice was tight and controlled and not... Delaney.

I missed what we'd had with a ferocity that caused a physical pain in my gut.

I crossed the street and turned toward the plaza. Soon, the town would light up every tree and storefront, creating a winter wonderland in Trickle Creek's annual Merry and Bright Night. But for now, Plot Twist was the only bright festive spot in the plaza, her front window display proudly boasting all things Christmas.

I couldn't help but smile at her commitment to the holidays, no matter what anyone else, myself included, said about it being too early.

Peaks & Brews seemed dull by comparison as I stepped through the doors. Not that anyone was complaining. There were a few tables of customers laughing and talking, enjoying their beers. Jeff, my assistant manager and best employee, was handling things behind the bar with a friendly smile for everyone.

He lifted his hand in greeting, but he must have read the expression on my face and left me alone as I moved to the far end of the bar and took a seat.

I spun around to take it all in. The brewery was everything I'd imagined it would be. Steady customers. A solid lineup of delicious brews. A positive bottom line.

But sitting there, alone, none of it felt the way it should have.

I leaned back against the smooth wood and crossed my arms.

Today had been just one more reminder about how badly I'd screwed up the best thing I'd ever had. I knew there was logic in waiting for the time to be right, and picking my moment and all of that. But I couldn't help but worry that the longer I waited, the higher the risk that I wouldn't be able to come back from my fuckup.

I couldn't risk it.

I pulled my phone from my back pocket and hit my brother's number.

"Reid," I said when he answered. "Where are you on that project?"

"I still have—"

"I need it finished." I cut him off. "Yesterday."

He blew out a breath that turned into a chuckle. "I can't go back in time, brother."

"Don't I know it," I muttered under my breath and then to Reid said, "I can come by the shop tomorrow and help. I need it done, Reid. As quickly as possible."

He was silent for a moment before I heard him blow out a breath. "Okay. I'll see what I can do about speeding things up. But I'm pretty sure having you lurking over my shoulder isn't going to make anything go any faster."

Chapter Twenty-Three

Delaney

The Tamarack Inn always felt like a warm hug. The moment I set foot inside the main lobby, I could smell something delicious mingling with the comforting, subtle scent of wood in the fireplace.

I shifted the canvas bag of books higher up on my shoulder and stamped the snow from my boots before tugging them off and leaving them on the rack by the front door.

Avery and Reid had done an amazing job with the renovation work on the inn, creating a welcoming space where both guests and locals liked to gather. There were a few people in the main room playing cards in front of the fireplace as I made my way to the back of the big house to the kitchen.

"Hey," Avery said from the stove when I walked in. "You made it."

"I sure did." I sat on a stool at the big island. "What are you cooking? It smells amazing."

"A toffee glaze for a coffee cake." She looked up at me as she continued stirring. "It will only be a moment. If I stop stirring, it'll burn."

"Don't worry about me," I told her. "I'm not in a hurry. Rochelle is watching the shop, and I have nowhere to be."

Avery flashed me a smile. "Then settle in. There's a fresh pot of coffee. Help yourself."

I made myself a cup and settled back into my spot, watching my friend as she masterfully glazed the coffee cake on the antique glass stand.

"I had no idea you were such a baker." I lifted my mug. "That looks incredible."

"Honestly, I've never been good at baking," she admitted. "But it turns out if you follow a recipe exactly, you have half a chance of it turning out edible."

I laughed. "That looks more than edible, Avery."

"I've been getting better." Avery shrugged. "As long as the guests like it, that's all that matters."

She stacked the dishes in the sink, poured herself a cup of coffee, and joined me at the counter.

"How's your holiday season looking?" I asked. "Are you booked up?"

"We are! It's incredible," she said. "Truthfully, this whole thing is exceeding even my wildest hopes. I couldn't be more thrilled."

I smiled warmly, happy for my friend. "You deserve it." I lifted the canvas tote and set it on the counter. "I brought you a selection of some of the most popular books in the shop right now."

"Thank you so much for bringing them over." Avery slid the bag over and pulled the books out. "I'll pop over and pay for these later."

"No rush." I waved her off. "I was happy for the excuse to get out of the shop for a bit."

And out of the plaza, I thought with a grimace. Having Ethan so close, yet so far away, was only getting harder instead of easier. It was ridiculous, but I couldn't stop staring at the wall we shared and remembering little things. Like how the dust had flown out of the duct the day I'd stormed over to his construction zone and confronted him. Had it really been so long ago?

Or when he sat in the chairs in the nook and told me why *Wheel of Time* had been his favorite series since he was young.

I needed to move past it. Besides, it was better that I figured out who Ethan really was before things got even more serious.

It was what I'd been telling myself, anyway. Even if I didn't quite believe it. Or believe it even a little bit.

I exhaled sharply and refocused on my friend, who was watching me with a concerned look. "Where is Reid today, anyway?"

It was the reason she said she couldn't get away from the inn, precipitating my trip to her with the books.

She smiled and waved a hand. "He's practically been living in his wood shop for the past few days."

"Really? What's he working on now?" Besides being the town handyman and helping Avery out with the inn, Reid had recently started up a fine woodworking business as well. He'd created many of the pieces in the inn, as well as Ethan's bar tops, and I knew his work was in high demand, but I hadn't heard about his latest project.

"I'm not really sure." Avery busied herself with the stack of books I'd brought, examining each title. "He didn't mention the details," she said vaguely.

I gave her a strange look, but she didn't notice.

"How are you doing?" she asked after a moment. "You know, with—"

"I'm fine." I pasted a fake smile on my face. "Just keeping busy. You know how it is."

"Delaney." Something in her smile shifted. "Seriously. Are you okay?"

I blinked. I did not want to talk about just how *not* okay I really was. "Of course. Why?"

"You just seem…" She shrugged. "Off."

"Ha." I set my mug down and folded my hands under my chin. "Yeah. Well, it's been a week."

"I heard about the fundraiser."

Of course she had. With Tilley at the helm, no doubt everyone in town had heard about the fundraiser and how Ethan and I had been stuck working together. Not for one second did I think that was an accident, either. If Tilley had hoped it would bring us back together somehow, no doubt she was desperately disappointed with how it had turned out.

"It was fine," I lied. "We sorted jackets and gloves. Made some small talk."

Avery tilted her head. "That's a good thing?"

"It's…not a bad thing, I guess."

"Do you think that you and Ethan…" she started and then bit her lip.

"Just say it."

"Okay." Avery nodded. "I was just going to ask you if you thought that you and Ethan would ever be able to get past what happened," she said quickly. "I mean, I know you're upset and you have every right to be." Avery held up a hand before I could interrupt. "I'd be mad, too."

I sucked in a breath.

"I was just thinking," Avery continued. "You two were so good together. Maybe he didn't realize that he'd...well...you know."

"I do know." I chose my words carefully. "And honestly, Avery, I wish we could get past it." I blinked back the tears that threatened. "I know it doesn't seem like a big thing to some people. But, you have to understand my past and how long it took me to get over my divorce and the fallout from it. With Ethan, I thought that we could...well, it doesn't matter what I thought. The thing is, I've been down that road before," I told her. "I've loved and trusted and lost everything and..." I swallowed hard. Ethan was *not* Ken. Logically, I knew that, but it was too hard to untangle the two in my head.

"Have you talked to him about everything?" Avery asked gently. "I bet if you heard him out, he'd—"

"That's the thing, Avery," I said sadly. "He hasn't even tried to talk to me about it. Or apologize, or even try to understand why I'm so hurt. And that...well, that hurts the most."

I looked down into my mug of coffee and took a moment, because that *was* the part that hurt the most. I really thought we were building something together, but he had just let me walk away. Like it never even mattered.

Avery slipped her hand over mine.

When I finally looked up into her kind eyes, I didn't try to stop the tear that slid down my cheek. "I'm just so tired," I said. "Tired of trying to pretend it's all okay, and I don't still want it to mean something to him."

She didn't push. She just let me sit while the tears fell. After a moment, she stood and wrapped her arms around me in a gentle hug. "It's okay," she said. "You don't have to pretend. Not with me, Delaney."

Ethan

"I knew you were going to be a pain in the ass," Reid grumbled without turning around. "You know, standing over me, watching everything I do, isn't going to make me move any faster, Ethan."

Reid turned and crossed his arms over his chest, glaring at me.

I knew I was taking a risk by popping into my brother's wood shop unannounced and unwelcome, but I could not sit at home or in the brewery for another moment just *waiting.*

"I'm losing my mind here, Reid. I can't just do nothing."

"That's a you problem," he growled. "I don't work with an audience," he told me. "So if you want me to finish this for you on the ridiculously tight timeline you've demanded of me, you need to go find something else to do."

I opened my mouth to say something but snapped it shut again. Arguing with Reid about how fast he was working on the piece I'd commissioned was definitely the wrong move. Even through my clouded brain, I could see that.

"Okay, okay. I hear you." I dragged a hand through my hair and took a step back from the workbench.

Reid grunted and picked up a rag. I watched while he ran it down the smooth edge of the piece, inspecting a tiny detail I couldn't see.

I shifted my weight and shoved my hands in my pockets. "You think she's going to like it?"

A sound dangerously close to a growl escaped my brother. "You already asked me that."

"You didn't answer."

He sighed. The kind that said he was only barely controlling his temper, which was impressive considering Reid was not known for holding back. Either he really did feel bad for me and my situation, or Avery had made a bigger impact on him than I realized.

He turned and ran a hand down the back side of the piece. "I think she's going to love it." He wiped a speck of dust I didn't see from the surface. "But that's not the point, and I think you know that."

I did.

I took a step closer, examining the piece Reid created based on my vision. The warm wood grain, the smooth beveled top, and the inlaid details of mountains and books on the front. It truly was a stunning front counter for Plot Twist. It was everything Delaney deserved.

"I just keep second-guessing myself," I confessed after a moment. "Will this be enough?"

"No," Reid said without hesitation. "This is a gesture. But it's not the solution. You know that, brother."

I did. I blew out a breath.

"But do you think it's too late?"

With an exasperated exhale, Reid set the rag down and turned. "Honestly? No. I don't."

I raised one brow and waited.

"I think she's hurt, Ethan. But she's not gone. Not yet, and I think you know that, which is why you're standing here, driving me crazy."

I chuckled and shook my head. "I never thought I'd see the day when I was relying on you for emotional insight, Reid."

That brought a smile to my brother's face. "Don't get used to it."

We stood there for a moment, the smell of wood stain and sawdust filling the space between us, before I finally said, "She's the one."

Reid's expression softened. After a moment, he nodded. "I know."

Before I could respond, he punched me in the shoulder. "So grab an end and get this loaded up and over to Delaney so I don't need to hear about it anymore."

Chapter Twenty-Four

Delaney

B y the time I made it back to the shop, the sun was dipping low, casting golden streaks across the snow-dusted plaza. I tugged my scarf tighter around my neck, more as a security mechanism than to keep out the chill that seemed to be seeping into every part of me.

I was beyond exhausted. And it wasn't just the long hours spent getting ready for the holiday season. Opening up to Avery, even if it was just a little bit, had left me wrung out. I felt like I could crawl into bed and sleep for days.

Lucky for me, Rochelle was scheduled for the rest of the night and would close up the shop.

The bells over the door gave their usual cheerful jingle as I stepped inside.

The familiar warmth of the shop wrapped around me. Instinctively, I moved to the front counter and set down the canvas bag with the books Avery didn't want, before shrugging out of my coat.

That's when I noticed it.

Or rather, I didn't notice it at first.

Something felt different.

I looked behind me, but didn't see Rochelle. I turned slowly back to the front counter and froze.

The old, rickety desk that I'd inherited when I bought the store—and was constantly propping up with an old book under one leg—was gone.

In its place was something new.

Something stunning.

A dark-stained wood, smooth and polished to a soft sheen. Clean, simple lines, with a gentle curve to stand behind.

Slowly, I moved to look at the front, and the inlay of the lighter wood, made to look like a mountain range with books. It was a piece of art.

I stepped closer, blinking in disbelief that this piece of furniture was in my shop. And that it looked as if it had always been there. Like it belonged.

My fingertips brushed along the edge before I even realized I was reaching out.

There was no doubt who'd crafted such an exceptional piece.

And just as I knew Reid Lyons had made the counter, I knew who'd commissioned it.

He'd heard me. He'd noticed.

He'd remembered.

My throat tightened, and hot tears stung my eyes.

Behind me, I heard movement, reminding me I wasn't alone.

I swiped at my eyes and spun around, expecting to see my employee.

"Quinn." I couldn't hide my surprise to see the girl standing there with an envelope in her hand. "What are you—"

"It's pretty nice, huh?" She jerked her head toward the counter.

I could only nod in reply.

"Here." She thrust the envelope at me and took a step back, waiting for me to open it.

I hesitated.

"Go on," Quinn said softly, rocking on her heels like she was trying to play it cool. "I'm not leaving until you do."

My hands shook as I slipped my finger under the flap and pulled out a single sheet of paper.

Delaney,

I can't undo what I did. And I won't pretend that a counter can erase how I made you feel. But I hope it will at least serve as enough of a peace offering that you will agree to hear me out.

Please come next door.

~Ethan

I STARED AT THE WORDS, reading them once and then again. My heart beat so loudly, I was sure Quinn could hear it.

"Well?"

I glanced up at her. "I—"

"I told him you'd come," she said, her voice quiet but determined. "You don't even have to say anything," she continued. "But if you don't go, then I'm going to have to deal with him, and I don't think I can handle that." She offered me a half smile and a shrug.

"Fair enough." I couldn't help but smile. "You're very bossy for a twelve-year-old, you know?"

"Only when it matters," she said seriously. "And this matters. A lot."

I sucked in a breath and nodded. "Okay."

"Don't worry about the shop," Quinn said. "I'll stay here and help Rochelle close up. And then I'll head over to Uncle Reid's for the night. He said something about a coffee cake."

My heart swelled, knowing how orchestrated this whole thing had been. But that didn't change...well...anything.

I looked back at the note. My fingers trembled a little as I folded it again.

Without another word, I slipped it into my coat pocket, nodded once to Quinn, and walked out the door.

Ethan

I'd gone over every detail a thousand times.

We'd arranged for Delaney to be at the inn all afternoon.

We'd delivered the countertop and put it exactly in place.

I shut the brewery early.

I sent everyone home.

I'd written the note.

I'd set everything up.

But still, I wasn't sure that she'd come.

Quinn promised that she'd make sure of it. I knew that it was playing dirty to get my daughter to make the request, but I also knew that Delaney wasn't likely to deny her. And I just needed her to get here so I could look into her eyes and tell her exactly how I felt.

Finally.

The brewery had never been this quiet. Not since the night before we'd opened.

No music.

No clinking glasses or happy chatter filling the air.

Only the light hum of the coolers and the soft flicker of candlelight cast shadows across the bar top.

I'd pushed back most of the tables in the main seating area and set up one small low table with an eclectic mix of candles on top and two oversized cushions on the floor, just like the ones we'd sat on in her living room during the snowstorm.

I had a crockpot behind the bar, keeping the homemade beef stew warm. But instead of a bottle of red wine, I had something different in mind.

I glanced out the front window again.

Still, there was no sign of her.

Avery texted when Delaney had left the inn. She should have been back at the shop at least ten minutes ago. *Had she seen the counter? Had she gotten the note?*

I paced the length of the shop and wiped my palms on my jeans.

What if she wasn't coming?

My heart thudded, slow and heavy.

What if it was too little, too late?

And then, the door opened.

I froze, and all the air escaped my lungs as she stepped inside.

Delaney.

Her hair was loose over her shoulders, her cheeks just a little pink from the cold…she looked beautiful. But uncertain, too. And vulnerable in a way that took my breath away.

"You came."

She pulled her hand out of her pocket. She was holding the note. "I wasn't given much of a choice," she said with a small smile. "Not fair sending in reinforcements."

"Sorry." I shrugged. "No," I added quickly. "I'm not. I needed to make sure you'd come."

The smile slipped off her face. "I'm here." She took a tentative step forward. "Thank you for the counter. It's...it's stunning, Ethan. I don't know how to thank you."

More than anything, I wanted to reach for her, but I didn't want to spook her. I needed to move slowly and with certainty. "You can thank me by taking your coat off and staying for a minute." I waved my arm behind me to encompass the table and the setup on the floor.

"Oh." She shook her head slowly. "I didn't expect this."

I waited while she walked toward the table and took it all in before she looked up. "Is that beef stew I smell?"

"It sure is." I held my hands out for her coat, which she gave me after a moment. "If you're hungry."

She hesitated, but only for a moment, before she said, "Honestly, what I could use is a drink."

There was no stopping me from grinning. "I'm so glad you said that," I told her. "Because I have just the thing." I gestured for her to follow me to the bar.

I draped her coat over a stool before moving behind the bar to the brand-new tap that had been installed. "I have a new brew I really want you to try." Before she could decline, I grabbed a pint glass and kept talking. "Truthfully, I've been working on this one for a while." I filled one glass and then a second. "I've been trying to find the right balance. It's bold.

A little stubborn and kind of soft and special at the same time."

She knitted her brows together and assessed me.

"But the best part is that it surprises you in the best possible way." I handed her a glass.

"All that in a beer?"

I nodded seriously. "Wait until you try it."

She gave me a skeptical look, but when I held my glass out, she met mine with her own in a clink and lifted it to her lips.

I took my own drink, but didn't take my eyes off her, wanting to see every second of her reaction.

Delaney swallowed and looked at me. "It's delicious."

"You sound surprised."

She chuckled a little. "You know, beer usually isn't my favorite."

"That's why I brewed this one," I told her. "Just for you."

She couldn't keep the surprise off her face. "For me."

"Well, more like for *us.*" I pointed to the new tap and the name that had been engraved on it.

Delaney leaned over to read it. "Chapter One?" She looked at me in question.

I held my breath for a moment before blowing it out. "As in, *our* chapter one," I told her. "Because there'll be many more chapters for us to write. Together." Her face changed, but I kept talking. "I mean, obviously I hope there'll be more chapters." I shrugged and forced myself to stop trying to overexplain. "Like I said, I've been working on it for a while. Before, I…well, before I screwed it all up."

Her eyes met mine.

"I should have told you about it earlier. I should have

shown you. I should have——" I stopped and forced myself to slow down. "I should have done a lot of things, Delaney. The truth is, I wasn't paying attention when it mattered most." I took a chance and reached for her hand.

She didn't immediately pull away, which I took to be a good sign.

"I know I hurt you because you thought I didn't consider you. And you're right," I added quickly before she could interject. "I *didn't.* Not in that moment. And that was not okay. I'm so sorry for that. I promise you, I will do everything in my power to make that right." I squeezed her hand. "But I need you to know that I *do* consider you. From the moment you walked into this brewery when it was little more than an old Chinese food restaurant full of dust and mess, I have considered you."

Her chin trembled slightly.

"You're in every plan I make. Every moment of my day. My every thought and feeling. Sometimes I think that you are *all* I consider. And I hope like hell that you will accept my apology for not showing up for you when you needed me to." I looked into her eyes. "Please believe me when I tell you that I will spend from now until the end of time trying to make it up to you if you let me."

I blew out a breath. Finished.

Delaney didn't speak right away.

Her eyes searched mine, as if she were trying to see whether the words I'd just spoken were real or another charm-laced, meaningless promise.

But I didn't look away. I couldn't. I needed her to believe that I meant what I said. All of it and so much more.

Delaney

His hand was warm in mine. It felt like an anchor keeping me from floating away.

It was the tether to reality I needed, because in that moment, nothing seemed real anymore.

The counter.

The beer.

The setup on the floor just like our first night together.

The way he was looking at me like I was the only thing in the world that mattered.

It was too much and exactly enough all at the same time.

"You really brewed a beer for us?" I asked softly.

"I did."

"And you commissioned a front counter for me."

A small smile twitched at the corner of his lips. "I'm going to owe Reid for a long time for that one."

I wanted to smile, too. But I was still so unsure. "Thank you," I said quietly. "For listening. For noticing."

"Of course." Ethan squeezed my hand. "I couldn't help but notice that rickety counter." He laughed a little. "You deserved so much more. You *do* deserve so much more."

I glanced down for a moment, finding the courage to say what I needed to. "You hurt me."

He sucked in a breath and when I looked up, I could see the pain all over his face. But he didn't try to interrupt me.

"It wasn't just about the patio," I continued, trying to keep my voice level. "Or the noise level, or the customers, or how it would affect Plot Twist."

He flinched. "I know."

"You do?"

He nodded. "You trusted me, and I let you down."

Ethan reached for my other hand and pulled them together, taking a step toward me. He pressed his hands to his chest. "If I could take it back, I would in a heartbeat. But I can't," he added softly. "All I can do now is try to convince you that it was a mistake and it won't happen again. And show you." He spun me a little to take in the romantic, and slightly cheesy, setup he'd created.

I laughed a little, despite myself. Because it *was* cheesy. But it was also the sweetest thing anyone had ever done for me. And the biggest part was, besides the table setup, he'd done it *before* our fight.

The beer.

The counter.

That stuff takes time.

He *had* considered me.

In the very sweetest way.

"You have shown me," I said. "This is…"

"The most romantic thing you've ever seen?" He wiggled his eyebrows, and I couldn't help but laugh.

"Yes," I answered honestly. "And the beer isn't half bad either."

"Ouch." Ethan pretended to be offended.

I dropped my eyes a little before looking up and meeting his gaze. "It's delicious," I told him honestly. "And the name…"

"You like it?"

"I love it. The first chapter is always so exciting. So full of promise and anticipation of what's to come."

"Like us?"

I tilted my head up to his and nodded slowly. "I hope so."

He stepped closer until we were only inches apart.

"Delaney," his voice was rough, "I need you to know that you matter to me." He spoke slowly. "You mattered then, and you matter now. So, *so* much. I screwed up, and I'll probably do it again. But I hope like hell you don't give up on me." He released my hands and cupped my cheeks instead, holding me in place while he spoke the words directly into my heart. "Because I am falling deeply and helplessly in love with you. And if you give me another chance, I promise I'll make sure you see and feel exactly how much you matter to me."

My heart flipped in my chest, and a tear slipped down my cheek. "I'm scared," I whispered truthfully, releasing the weight of it in my chest. "I've given too much once before and I lost everything. I can't…"

"You won't," he said, his voice confident and strong. "Because this is different. It's real."

I believed him, because I felt it, too. The last few weeks without him had felt wrong, like I was missing a big part of myself.

After a moment, I nodded. "This is chapter one."

The smile that took over his face lit me up inside. "And we have an entire book to write together, sweetheart."

Then he was kissing me, and everything felt right again.

When he finally pulled back, I smiled. "You're pretty cheesy for a beer guy."

He laughed. "I believe the word you're looking for is *romantic*." He took my hand and led me to the table in the middle of the room. But before I sat, he spun me into his arms one more time. "I meant what I said, Delaney. This is just the start of our story. I can't wait to see what happens next."

I winked and bit my bottom lip. "Oh, I think I have a pretty good idea what will happen next."

His eyes grew wide, and I laughed. "But first, how about another taste of that new brew? And that stew smells delicious."

Chapter Twenty-Five

Ethan

The room was quiet, the only light coming from the lamp on Delaney's nightstand. Outside, snow had started to fall softly, but inside, everything was warm and cozy. And perfect.

Delaney's hair was fanned over the pillow, her leg draped loosely over mine. Her fingers traced light circles over my chest like she didn't even realize she was doing it.

After another pint of Chapter One and a bowl of stew, we'd left the brewery and slipped up to her apartment through the backstairs where we couldn't be spotted and had been wrapped up in each other ever since.

"I still can't believe you named a beer after us." She propped herself up on one arm, her hair cascading over her naked breasts.

It took all my restraint not to pull her back into me for another kiss.

"What else are you going to name after me?"

I laughed. "Well, I was considering naming my next stout Stubborn as Hell."

She swatted me gently, and I pulled her back down to my chest and wrapped her up in my arms. "Or maybe we can pick out a name for the next one together?"

"I like that," she murmured against my chest.

A moment of quiet passed between us before she spoke again. "So...what now?"

I took a breath and released her enough so she could slip to my side, and we could look at each other. "Now, we figure this out," I said. "One thing at a time."

"Day by day?"

I nodded. "I don't have a perfect plan, but I want to do this right, Delaney. With you."

"I'd like that, too." She looked at me thoughtfully. "But what does that look like?"

I exhaled slowly. "Let's start with the obvious. The patio."

She flinched a little, a gentle reminder that at least for the moment, the patio was still a sore spot.

"I've already reworked my plan," I told her. "The tables won't infringe on the space in front of your shop. And I even asked Grayson for some ideas on how to put together a planter barrier that will make sure not to interfere with your window displays."

"You reworked it?"

"Yeah," I said. "Because you were right. I didn't think it through the first time. Not properly anyway."

"But won't that take away business from you?"

I shook my head and grinned. "That's the best part," I told her. "I'm going to use this as an experiment. And if it's popular, I can expand the space in the back to a proper patio space next summer. It won't impact your shop at all, and it'll be a good use of space. I can even offer up some live music from time to time. Acoustic, of course," I added quickly. "Nothing that will cause a disruption."

She went quiet, thinking it through. After a moment, she nodded and smiled slowly. "I really like that plan. You thought about it."

"With you in mind. Every step of the way."

"And Quinn?"

I blinked. "I don't think she'll care about the patio one way or the other." I grinned.

"That's not what I mean, and you know it." She shook her head. "I meant, what about…well…I don't want her to get hurt again."

"She won't," I said quickly. "Because you and me…"

I didn't finish the thought, but I didn't need to.

"I still think we need to move slowly," Delaney said. "Ease her into whatever this…"

"Agreed." It was exactly what I'd been thinking. "But you and I both know, she'll have a much different idea of how we should move."

That made Delaney laugh. "Truth."

We lay there for another few seconds without talking. Just breathing together in an easy rhythm.

Eventually, Delaney spoke again. "This doesn't have to be perfect."

"No," I agreed. "Just honest."

"I can do honest." She rolled onto her side so she faced me fully before she said, "In the spirit of being honest, I didn't say it before. But in case it's not evident by now, I'm falling in love with you, too."

Warmth spread under my rib cage, filling me in the best possible way. "I can't tell you how happy I am to hear that. But since we're doing this honest thing," I said, "I need to admit that I'm not actually falling in love with you, Delaney."

Her eyes flashed, and I tried not to smile as I continued quickly. "I'm not falling, because I'm already there." I cupped her cheek, stroking my thumb gently over her soft skin. "I have truly and completely fallen in love with you."

Her face transformed. "Are you saying that you love me, Ethan Lyons?"

I chuckled and pulled her on top of me. "I am madly and desperately in love with you, Delaney Hart."

She laughed while I kissed her, but it didn't take long before that laughter turned into small moans, and then into something quieter—deeper—as we lost ourselves in each other once again. The rest of the world and all our plans could wait.

Because, at least for the night, it was only the two of us.

Chapter Twenty-Six

DECEMBER 1ST

Ethan

"It's officially Christmas!" Quinn grabbed the end of the gaudiest red and silver garland I'd ever seen and started to run through the brewery with it.

I shook my head and tried to hide my smile. My daughter had been counting down the days until I'd finally let her decorate for the holidays. Despite a tag team effort with her and Delaney, I'd held firm to my December first date.

"It's not Christmas," I called after her. "It's December."

"Same same," Delaney said with a wink as she walked past me, carrying a giant wreath.

"Where is *that* going?"

"Don't worry about it," Delaney said. "We've got this."

"Yeah, Dad," Quinn echoed her. "We've got this."

"Yeah, Ethan," Preston said with a laugh. "They've got this." I shot him a look, but he only laughed harder. "What do you have on tap that's festive?"

I knew when I'd been beaten. I moved behind the bar,

which was where it was safest for me, and pulled Preston a pint. "It's not festive, but it's our best seller these days."

"Chapter One." Preston grinned into his glass before taking a big gulp. "It is a winner."

He spun on his stool to watch the chaos taking place in the brewery.

It looked like all things Christmas had exploded onto every table. At least all things tinsel and over-the-top gaudy Christmas. Where Delaney's store had a distinct rustic holiday theme with pine boughs, pine cones, and tasteful bows, everything she'd brought over to Peaks & Brews was silver and red and...shiny.

"Good for you, letting her run with things, man." Preston shook his head.

"Hey. It makes them happy." I joined him and pulled up a stool. "And if my girls are happy, I'm happy."

Preston turned to me with a raised brow. "Your *girls*? It's like that, is it?"

I nodded once. Without a doubt, it was.

"Pretty serious then?"

"Like a heart attack," I said, and then quickly added, "Only way better."

My younger brother laughed so hard, he almost choked on his beer. "I'm glad to hear it, Ethan," he said when he'd recovered. "Delaney's awesome."

"She sure is."

"Even if her taste in decorations for this place is questionable."

I couldn't disagree with that.

The bells over the door announced Grayson's arrival, along with a gust of cold air and a giant pine tree. "Ho ho ho!"

At least I was pretty sure it was Grayson. The tree was massive.

"No, no, no!" I jumped up from my stool. "You need to get that out of here."

"Dad!" Quinn was at my side, Delaney right behind her. Both of them stared at me. "It's a Christmas tree," Quinn said. "We *need* a Christmas tree."

"*We* do," I told her. "The brewery does not."

"Are you sure about that, Ethan?" Delaney was trying her best not to smile. "I mean, are you even properly decorated for Christmas without a tree?"

I opened my mouth to object, but she continued quickly.

"I thought maybe you could decorate it with those new cans you had made up for the beer. It's like advertising and decorating all in one."

"Yeah, Dad." Quinn crossed her arms.

Grayson peered around the tree and looked at me, his eyes sparkling with laughter. "Yeah, Ethan."

I was smart enough to know I wasn't going to win that particular argument. I threw up my arms. "Fine. The tree can stay."

Quinn clapped in delight while Delaney took over directing Grayson on where to put the largest Christmas tree I'd ever seen.

I rejoined Preston at the bar and tried to ignore his laughter.

A few minutes later, Avery and Reid joined us, each carrying cardboard boxes. I only shook my head at the number of decorations that continued to accumulate.

"This is…impressive," Reid said once he'd joined us at the bar.

Grayson was right behind him, leaving the women to

handle the decorating. I pulled them each a pint, and got Preston and me fresh ones.

"I was promised pasta and pizza for my efforts," Reid said as he took the glass with a nod of thanks.

"Brody's picking it up on his way over."

Right on cue, the door opened once more, and Lauren and Brody walked through, laden down with take-out boxes from Willa's Whisk across the plaza.

Delaney

My stomach growled at the mouthwatering aroma of garlic bread and roasted tomato sauce, the second Lauren and Brody walked in with arms full of takeaway containers.

I'd been so busy Christmasfying the brewery, I hadn't realized how hungry I was.

"This looks amazing," I said as I joined everyone else at the counter.

Ethan slipped an arm around my waist and pulled me in for a quick kiss.

"*You* look amazing." He tugged on the garland I had wrapped around my neck like a scarf. "I like you in tinsel."

Preston groaned and Grayson laughed when I blushed. I did a quick scan for Quinn, lest she see us being *gross*. But she was still digging through a box, pulling out sparkly ornaments.

"This is amazing," Reid said with a moan as he took a bite of pizza. "Did Willa change the recipe? I mean, it's always been good, but this is…"

"Heavenly," Preston finished for him with a mouthful of spaghetti.

Grayson raised an eyebrow at his word choice, but Preston shrugged and said, "Seriously. It's damn good."

"I'm not going to take your word for it." Grayson filled a plate and tucked in, agreeing with his brother's assessment almost at once. "Damn. You're not wrong. This is next level."

"Right?" Lauren said. "It must be Harper's tweaks. That woman is not playing around. I ate there the other day, and I swear, all of a sudden, that diner is like a Michelin star— what?"

Everyone had grown still and was staring at Lauren.

"What?" she asked again, just as oblivious as I was as to what she'd said wrong. "You all must know Harper, right? She's Willa's—"

"We know who she is." Ethan cut her off gently and shot Grayson a quick look before turning his attention back to Lauren. "We went to school with her."

I looked around the group. I sometimes forgot that Lauren didn't grow up in Trickle Creek.

"Then why are you—"

"Harper's back?"

I whipped around to see Grayson, who looked as if he'd seen a ghost.

He set his hardly touched plate on the counter and pushed it away. "Did you know?" He directed the question to Brody.

The eldest Lyons brother shrugged in an effort to look casual. "I just found out when I picked up the food. She said to say hi."

Grayson was quiet for a moment before turning to me. His face was impossible to read. "Do you have lights for that tree?"

I nodded. "I sure do. I'll show you."

After I dug out a few tangled strands of lights and gave them to Grayson, who'd become much quieter than I'd ever seen him, I returned to my uneaten dinner and the rest of the group.

"Does anyone want to tell me what that was all about?"

Ethan handed me a piece of garlic bread. "They were a thing in high school."

"Not just a *thing*," Reid said with a shake of his head. "She was the great love of his life. At least, that's how Gray sees it."

"So…" I glanced behind me, where Reid's twin was busy stringing the lights with Quinn's help. "Obviously, it didn't end well?"

"That's the thing." Preston shrugged. "It's not like it ended dramatically or anything. I mean, Grayson's not really the drama type."

There were a few chuckles. Grayson was probably the steadiest and most drama-free of all the brothers.

I pulled up a stool and picked up my fork. The pasta *really* was good.

"Harper always dreamed of going to culinary school and working around the world," Ethan explained as I ate. "Grayson wanted a small-town life."

"So he broke up with her?" I quickly filled in the blanks.

Ethan nodded. "It broke his heart."

"And he's never really dated since," Reid added. "Not seriously, anyway."

"Wow."

"Yeah," Brody agreed with me. "Wow."

"And now she's back," I said.

Preston shrugged. "No idea for how long."

"Huh." I couldn't help but smile, the inner romantic in me automatically playing out a dozen scenarios for Grayson. "Sounds like it could get complicated."

"It sure does," Avery said. "I hope it's—"

"Are you all going to sit around and talk about me all day?" Grayson yelled from the other side of the brewery, interrupting the conversation. "Or can we get some help with this tree?"

Reid laughed and shook his head. "Relax," he fired back. "We haven't even gotten to the good part yet."

Grayson shook his head, but Reid jumped up to help him and just like that, the conversation was over.

With the whole group, decorating went even faster than I expected, and it wasn't long before my theme of red and silver glitter with just a touch of *beer* was complete.

"I have to admit," Ethan wrapped an arm around my waist, "I had my doubts about this, but…"

"It's pretty great."

"You're pretty great." He spun me so I was in his arms, my lips only inches from his. "I'm really glad you're here."

"I'm really glad to be here," I murmured before pressing my lips to his.

"Ewww." Quinn appeared out of nowhere, just the way she always seemed to whenever we tried to sneak a kiss. "You guys are *so* gross."

I pulled back just in time to see her roll her eyes, but her bright smile betrayed how she really felt.

"It just so happens I like being gross with Delaney." Ethan kissed me again, and I laughed when Quinn groaned loudly.

"I like being gross with you, too," I said with a wink when we pulled apart.

"Fine." Quinn stretched out the word. "I guess I'd rather the two of you be gross instead of stupid."

"Stupid?"

"Yeah," Quinn responded to her dad with a shake of her head. "You know, like when you guys weren't talking because of something dumb? And you were walking around pretending you didn't love each other, but really you were just making the rest of us crazy? That kind of stupid."

I couldn't help but laugh. For a twelve-year-old, she really was wiser than her years.

"You're right, Quinn." With one arm still around Ethan, I opened my other one for her. She slipped easily into our arms and all together, we squeezed tight. "Gross is *way* better than stupid."

I closed my eyes and soaked in the moment before Quinn wiggled her way out of our embrace and ran off to check on the symmetry of the tree.

I leaned into Ethan's side. He placed an easy kiss on the top of my head but didn't say anything.

Neither did I.

But for the first time in a long time, I wasn't wondering what came next.

I was already in it.

Epilogue

Delaney

It was warm for a spring evening in the mountains. But after what felt like a very long winter, I'd take any indication that summer was well and truly on its way.

The air in the plaza held the freshly sweet scent of the dogwoods that were in full white bloom in the oversized planter beds. The town had recently planted some bright annuals in the gardens as well. A sign of confidence that there shouldn't be any late-season snowstorms.

The patio at Peaks & Brews was buzzing with conversation and the low hum of acoustic music as I made my way next door.

It had only been open a few weeks, but already the outdoor seating was proving to be a massive hit. The patio had been packed every night, and Ethan was already talking about going ahead with plans to develop the space in the back to accommodate more seating.

I had to admit, he'd done an amazing job creating a welcoming space that didn't detract from Plot Twist. If anything, the big planters of flowers and string lights that crossed overhead, gently illuminating the space, only enhanced the feel of my own shop.

At the same time that Peaks & Brews had opened the outdoor seating, I'd added a sitting area of my own. Two big cushioned armchairs with a little wrought-iron table between them and a few flower pots from Charli's shop were set outside the front windows.

The seating was already getting used more than I'd expected, and I'd considered looking for a few more chairs for customers to enjoy.

"I swear," Lauren said as she joined me in the plaza. "You've got half the town reading again with this setup." She wrapped an arm around my shoulders and squeezed.

"I don't know if it's the books or the beer." I laughed. "Okay, that's not true. I'm sure the beer helps *a lot*."

"Whatever it is," my friend smiled, "it's amazing what you've created here. What you've *both* created."

She wasn't wrong. It was amazing. When Ethan and I had first come up with the idea of Books & Brews, to spin off the table we'd had at the Fall into the Plaza event, we weren't sure it would work as a regular activity, so we started small.

It was a pairing night where Ethan put together a curated flight of beers to match up with five books that I selected.

People loved it.

Like, *really* loved it.

We'd been blown away at the reception of the event, including how many people bought books to go home with, as well as six-packs of the new cans Ethan had started to produce.

Not only was the event a lot of fun, but it had been

successful, too. Everyone in attendance asked about when the next one would be, and word got around so quickly that we had to limit seating.

"I'm glad we can expand outside now." I looked around. Ethan had the big garage door windows open, creating the perfect inside-to-outside space he'd dreamed of. The entire brewery was packed.

"Do you guys have a table?" I asked Lauren.

"You know we do." She grinned. "I brought Brett tonight."

"Brett?" My eyes scanned the brewery, looking for her table. It didn't take long for my gaze to land on a small table with a man who must be Brett and a very sour-looking Brody, who was nursing the beer in front of him. "Who's Brett? And why does Brody look so pissed?"

"Brett and I have sort of been dating." Lauren shrugged in an effort to be casual, but it didn't work. I saw the way she bit her bottom lip and glanced away when she spoke. "I don't know what Brody's issue is."

I raised an eyebrow. "I think I know very well what his issue is."

She shook her head. "It's not like Brody and I are dating."

"Right." I dragged out the word. I'd been friends with Lauren for a while now, and I'd seen the two of them together more often than not, and I still couldn't figure out what was going on between the two of them. But she was correct—they weren't dating. As for the exact status of their actual relationship, I had no idea.

I let my eyes travel inside, where Ethan was behind the bar, filling pint glasses and grinning from ear to ear.

My stomach flipped, and a smile of my own took over my face.

"Go." Lauren elbowed me gently in the ribs. "I won't keep you."

I gave my friend a quick hug before attempting to pick my way through the crowd to my man. I didn't get far when Avery stopped me.

"There you are."

"Is something wrong?"

She laughed. "Only that Reid is losing his mind." Avery grabbed me by the elbow and steered me to a small table where Reid sat, glowering over his beer.

"What..." I looked between Avery and Reid, my concern growing. "What's wrong, Reid?"

"That." He jabbed his finger out, and I followed where he pointed to see Quinn with a table of friends in the far corner, with a pile of books stacked in front of them.

I looked back at Reid in question.

"He's mad because Quinn is over there flirting with boys."

I laughed out loud, but when Reid glared at me, I did my best to swallow it. Avery winked at me.

"Quinn's thirteen now," I told her overprotective uncle. "You were at the party, remember?"

We'd hosted a big party at Ethan's—well, *our* house in March. Only a few weeks after I moved in. "It's pretty normal for girls her age to be interested in boys."

Reid grumbled something under his breath and lifted his beer to his lips.

"You'll be okay." Avery patted his shoulder.

"Just think of Quinn as good practice for when you have your own one day."

Reid's mouth dropped open, and he stared at me in shock. "I think your daughter is all I can handle right now."

Daughter.

Quinn? My daughter?

The word struck me speechless. It took me a minute to recover.

"I mean, she's not…"

Avery put her hand on my shoulder and squeezed. "Yes," she said when I looked up at her. "She kinda is."

I took a breath and looked at Reid, who smiled for the first time and gave me a nod.

I exhaled slowly. "Okay," I said. "I guess she is a little bit mine." Saying it out loud made me smile.

I looked over at the table where she was laughing and joking with friends. And yes, also flirting. I couldn't help but laugh.

God, I loved that kid.

And Ethan. My eyes moved once more to the man behind the bar.

I loved this whole chaotic and totally unexpected life we were building together.

"Go," Avery said. "I'll try to talk Uncle Reid here off the ledge."

Ethan

It had been one of those nights that reminded me exactly why I'd wanted to start a brewery in the first place. Peaks & Brews had become one of the most popular gathering places in Trickle Creek, and that made me happier than I could ever have expected.

Of course, I was pretty sure Delaney had something to do with that happiness, too.

Just as I was thinking of her, I caught sight of my gorgeous girlfriend making her way through the crowd again. She'd already been waylaid by Lauren and then Avery. I had no doubt someone else would stop to talk to her.

Everyone loved Delaney.

Just not as much as I did.

Her hair was up, with only a few loose strands curling around her jaw. She looked relaxed and ready for the warmer weather with just a blouse and jeans on. It didn't matter what she wore—even in that ridiculous oversized sweater that she seemed to favor, Delaney always looked stunning.

I was a lucky man.

For so many reasons.

I still couldn't believe she lived with us now. Like a proper family. It had felt right for her to move out of her little apartment and into the house with us. Especially when she started spending more nights there than not.

I'd been concerned that Quinn might struggle with the transition, but she'd only seemed to thrive with a female role model around. The two of them got along so well, sometimes I felt like the odd man out.

But I didn't mind. Not really. I wouldn't trade life with my girls for anything.

Delaney reached the bar just as I'd finished pouring two pints, passing them off to a server.

"Hey there, beautiful." I wiped down the counter with a towel. "I didn't think you were ever going to make your way over here."

"Sorry. I got intercepted." She tilted her head toward Reid's table, where my brother sat, looking as if he'd just sucked on a sour pickle. "There was a Quinn situation."

"Let me guess." I grinned. "Boys?"

"Apparently."

"I should probably be more concerned," I said. "But I have no doubt that girl can hold her own. Besides, I'm still kind of stuck on the fact that she'd share her books with someone else."

"Right?" Delaney laughed. "The boy must be at least a little bit okay if she'd share her books with him."

She reached across the bar, her hand slipping over mine. "Do you have time for a break?"

"Actually, I do." I waved to my assistant manager, Jeff, and quickly pulled two pints of our favorite brew before joining Delaney.

Together, we slipped out to the back. One day, hopefully soon, we'd develop the space into a backyard deck space with more tables. But for the moment, it served as a quiet break spot.

I set the beers on the table and pulled out a chair for Delaney.

"It's nice and quiet out here," she said. "Perfect."

"I agree. As much as I love the chaos inside, this is nice."

"Chapter One?" She raised an eyebrow in question.

"Of course." It was our favorite brew for good reason.

"That's perfect." She lifted her glass. "It feels like a good night for a toast."

I picked up mine too. "To what?"

"To the life we're building," she started, her eyes meeting mine. "To where it started and where it's going."

"I like that."

We clinked glasses, and I took a sip. But she hesitated a moment before setting her glass down.

"Something wrong?"

"Not at all." She shook her head. "I was just thinking… it might be time for a new beer soon."

"Why is that?"

"Chapter One is over now, don't you think?"

"True…" I watched her carefully.

Delaney gave a quiet laugh and reached for my hand. Her expression softened slightly. "And…it looks like we're about to start a whole new chapter."

I searched her eyes, trying to figure out what the hell she was talking about and then—

"What?"

She smiled shyly.

"You mean—"

"Yup." She nodded. "I took two tests just to be sure."

I stared at her, my heart in my throat, not totally able to wrap my head around what was happening. "You're pregnant?"

"I am."

And just like that, it all became completely real.

I blinked and my mouth dropped open, but I couldn't find any words.

She gave me a second. "I know we didn't plan it and…I'm on birth control, so I'm not even totally sure how—"

I was already up, out of my chair and kneeling next to her before she could finish.

Her breath caught as I took her hand and kissed it, before looking her in the eyes. "I love you, Delaney. And this is the best news that I didn't even know I needed."

She let out a slow, shaky breath. "You're not freaking out?"

"Oh. I'm freaking out," I said with a laugh. "But in the best possible way."

She laughed then, and tears slipped down her cheeks.

I stood and pulled her up with me into my arms.

We stood like that for a long moment, just holding each other and enjoying the moment and everything it meant.

Eventually, I leaned down and whispered in her ear. "You know what this means, right?"

She tilted her head up, eyes questioning. "What?"

"That new brew... It's going to have to be non-alcoholic."

"I like that." Her smile was slow.

"I had a name idea."

She arched a brow.

"New Edition."

Her breath caught, just for a second. "It's perfect."

I kissed her then, with all the noise of the brewery and our family and friends in the background.

We'd started with chapter one.

And now, it was time to write a story that would last a lifetime.

**Go with Delaney, Ethan and Quinn for their first ultrasound appointment in an exclusive bonus scene.
Click HERE for that scene!**

**Willa's Whisk has always been the place to eat in Trickle Creek, but when Grayson Lyons learns that Willa's granddaughter Harper—his first love—is back at the resturant, things really start to heat up.
Grayson's story is next in <u>Fake It 'Till We Fall.</u>**

Have you caught up with all the Trickle Creek books?
Don't miss Reid and Avery's story, From Grumpy to Forever.
Join your favorite characters and start at the beginning with Never Let Me Go.

Bonus Scene

FOUR MONTHS LATER...

Delaney

"But what's it going to look like?" Quinn grabbed my arm. "I mean, will it look like *me?* Or like a squishy potato?"

"A squishy potato?" Ethan tried not to laugh from his chair across the tiny waiting room. "The baby is *not* going to look like a potato. Squishy or otherwise."

"Well, I don't know." Quinn looked to me for help, but I only shook my head. "This is my first baby."

I didn't even try to hide my little smile.

We waited until we had the pregnancy confirmed by the doctor before we told Quinn she was going to be a big sister.

Just as Ethan and I expected, she was instantly over-the-top excited and started making plans for the baby and wanted to be involved in every aspect, so it only felt right that we brought her along to our ultrasound appointment.

"This is my first baby, too." I put my hand over hers and squeezed. "But I don't think it's going to look like a squishy potato."

Quinn nodded, satisfied for the moment. She picked up

the book she'd been pretending to read, but I didn't miss the way her leg bounced and her eyes kept darting to the closed door.

My eyes met Ethan's from across the room. He looked like he wanted to laugh, but was doing a decent job of keeping it all together.

"If you've changed your mind about coming in—"

"Are you kidding?" Quinn almost jumped out of her chair. "I'm not going to miss seeing my baby sister for the first time."

"Or brother," Ethan said.

"It's a girl." Quinn crossed her arms. "I know it's a girl."

Father and daughter looked at me, but I only shrugged. It had been an ongoing debate in our house almost from the moment we told Quinn about the baby.

She was positive we were having a girl. And Ethan was sure it was a boy.

I had had no idea either way, and truthfully, I didn't care. I still sometimes had to pinch myself that we were having a baby at all, because it was definitely not part of the plan. Not that I didn't want to have children...someday—I did. But I'd been on the Pill for years, so it wasn't something I'd considered as an immediate possibility.

As it turned out, there was no such thing as one hundred percent foolproof birth control.

Once we got over the shock of it, Ethan and I were both thrilled and a little bit terrified.

"I already have names picked out," Quinn informed us.

"We are not naming the baby after a character in whatever fantasy novel you're reading, Quinn."

I snorted, then immediately tried to cover it when the nurse opened the door and called my name.

Ethan jumped up to help me out of my chair even

though I didn't need it, and placed a hand on the small of my back. His other hand instinctively reached for Quinn's shoulder, steadying her as she stood. None of us said anything as we followed the nurse into the dim room and got set up.

Once I was on the bed, a sheet draped over my belly, it all started to feel really real.

Quinn stood where she was placed at the end of the bed, her arms crossed, staring intently at the technician who was preparing for the exam.

The technician gave us a friendly greeting and briefly explained how everything was going to proceed.

"How are you doing?" Ethan asked as he sat in the chair next to me.

"I'm nervous," I admitted quietly.

"Same."

"You don't look nervous."

"I'm a really good actor." He reached for my hand, and we laced our hands together. His touch calmed me.

And then the screen lit up.

I'd seen ultrasound photos before, but nothing prepared you for the moment when that image appeared and you saw your very own baby for the first time in real time.

Our baby, impossibly tiny, and incredibly real, moving on the screen. The most amazing movie I'd ever seen.

"Whoa!" I couldn't take my eyes off the screen, but I had no doubt that Quinn's mouth was hanging open.

"Oh my God," I whispered.

"There's baby," the technician said as she moved the wand around my belly. "Nice strong heartbeat... An arm here....and there's another. Look at the fingers. Baby's waving to you."

"She's so cute."

"Or he," Ethan said.

"Do you want to know?" The technician froze, her wand stilled as she waited for our response.

Ethan and I looked at each other, and I nodded. "We do," I told her with a smile.

"Sounds good." She winked. "Let's see if baby will cooperate."

Quinn leaned in closer, squinting at the screen. "What am I looking for?"

The tech chuckled a little. "It can be hard to see, but... oh." She paused and looked up at Ethan and me. "It looks like you're going to have a girl."

I let out the breath I'd been holding. *A girl.*

"Yes! I knew it!"

Ethan was silent for a long moment. Then he cleared his throat. "Wow. A girl."

"Are you *crying*, Dad?"

"Are *you* crying?" he shot back, his voice rough.

"I'm crying because you're crying." She grabbed a tissue from the counter and moved around to stand beside her dad.

I laughed, which made the technician laugh. Ethan lifted my hand to his lips and wiped at his eyes when he thought no one was looking.

"She doesn't look like a squishy potato." Quinn leaned closer to the screen, examining her baby sister. "More like a peanut."

"She's perfect," I whispered.

"Damn right she is."

"You're so loved, baby girl." Tears slipped down my cheeks as the tech finished up and printed a few pictures.

She wiped the gel from my belly and left us alone.

Ethan helped me sit up and then bent to rest his forehead against mine. "You doing okay?"

"So much better than okay."

Quinn stood by the door, staring at the photos in her hand. "I'm not saying she's already my favorite person, but...yeah. She totally is my favorite person."

"You're going to be an excellent big sister," Ethan said.

"She's totally going to be my little minion." Quinn laughed, and I shook my head as we stepped out of the little room.

"It might be a few years before she's at the minion stage," I told her.

"That's okay." Quinn grinned at me. "I'm patient."

We all laughed because we knew that wasn't true at all.

"Come on," Ethan said. "Let me take my girls—all my girls," he added with his hand on my belly, "out for ice cream."

About the Author

Elena Aitken is a USA Today Bestselling Author of more than sixty romance and women's fiction novels. The mother of 'grown up' twins, Elena now lives with her very own mountain man in the heart of the very mountains she writes about. She can often be found with her toes in the lake and a glass of wine in her hand, dreaming up her next book and working on her own happily ever after.

To learn more about Elena:
www.elenaaitken.com
elena@elenaaitken.com

www.ingramcontent.com/pod-product-compliance
Lightning Source LLC
Chambersburg PA
CBHW031025260626
47153CB00017B/2128